Just Plain Bob

In My Wife's
Panties

10 Hot
Stories
in 1

Erotica Short Stories, Vol. 5

WARNING

This book contains sexually explicit scenes and adult language. It may be considered offensive to some readers. This book is for sale to adults ONLY.

* * * * * * * * * * * * * * * * * * *

Please store your files wisely where they cannot be accessed by underage readers.

Please feel free to send me an email. Just know that these emails are filtered by my publisher. Good news is always welcome.

Just Plain Bob - **justplainbob@awesomeauthors.org**

About the Publisher

4Fun Publishing, a member of **BLVNP Incorporated**, 340 S. Lemon #6200, Walnut CA 91789, info@blvnp.com / legal@blvnp.com
NOTE: Due to the highly emotional reaction of some people to works of erotic fiction, any email sent to the above address that contains foul language or religious references is automatically deleted by our anti-spam software and will not be seen. All other communications are welcome.

DISCLAIMER

Please don't be stupid and kill yourself. This book is a work of FICTION. Do not try any new sexual practice that you find in this book. It is fiction and not to be confused with reality. Neither the author nor the publisher or its associates assume any responsibility for any loss, injury, death or legal consequences resulting from acting on the contents in this book. Every character in this book is over 18 years of age. The author's opinions are not to be construed as the opinions of the publisher. The material in this book is for entertainment purposes ONLY. Enjoy.

Erotica Short Stories, Vol. 5

In My Wife's Panties

10 Hot Stories in 1

By: Just Plain Bob

© **Just Plain Bob 2015**
ISBN: 978-1-68030-264-6

Table of Contents

-
-
-
-
-
-
-

Karen's Repairman

-
-
-
-
-
-
-

These afternoon card games are getting out of hand thought Karen as her fingers slipped under the table, her cards forgotten. First one finger, then two as she listened to her friend Becky. The fingers slid in easily, her pussy already wet from the visions that Becky's story conjured up. She could just see it happening to Becky as Becky described it.

"I looked him up and down and saw the tent in his trousers and then I just said, "Sure honey, why not. I've never fucked a nigger before."

"Oh my god, you didn't really say that, did you?" squealed Alice.

"Damned straight I did. A guy so bold as to walk right up to you and say, "I want to fuck you" needs to be set back on his heels a little and if you want to shove back at a black man you call him a nigger."

"Is…is it true?" asked Connie from across the table. "I mean about how black guys are supposed to be hung?"

"Oh yeah, at least in his case it was true. His cock was every bit of nine inches long and it felt great in my pussy, but he didn't know how to use the thing. It was get on, get off and then pull out and wait for me to say something like "Oh god, you are just so masterful and thank you for giving me your cock." I guess I was supposed to be grateful. It was tasty though."

"Tasty?" asked Collette.

"Sure. I went down on him. He was such a lousy fuck that I had to do something to get myself off. I took that huge piece of meat in my mouth and gave him a blow job he'll never forget."

Sweet Jesus, thought Karen as the image of a large black man with an enormous cock appeared in her mind. It didn't even matter to her if Becky was lying or not. Just the thought of going down on a man, any man, was enough to make her cum.

The card games had started out innocently enough. Just a bunch of women with little to do and trying to find a way to make the day pass a little faster, but they had quickly deteriorated into bitch sessions. They started in on their husbands - how the men climbed on, fucked until they had cum and then rolled off and fell asleep. Then someone, Karen couldn't even remember who, had started talking about her extra-marital affairs. Then the other girls, one by one, had started telling of their extra-curricular activities. Karen had lied. She had never been fucked by any man other than her husband Jack, but for some strange reason she was ashamed to admit that to her friends. She had made up a story about a steamy affair that she'd had when Jack was out of town. Even though the story was fiction Karen still got wet when she thought about it and wished to God that it had been true. She had lied so it was possible that the other girls were lying also, but that didn't change anything. The tales, true or false, made her horny and made her long for the real thing. Karen had been fairly content for the first few years of her marriage, but the last four years had been frustrating for her. She needed more than just simple in and out fucking. She loved the feel of Jack driving furiously into her pussy, but he never gave her enough.

Driving home, Karen's mind kept replaying Becky's story in her head. She wondered what it would be like to give herself to a stranger; to go to her knees in front of a black man and suck him off the way Becky said she had. Jack didn't like oral sex - giving or getting - and he would never give in to Karen's entreaties to try it at least once. Once he had tried anal sex, but had decided that it was too degrading and he would never do it again. Karen wanted to experiment. She had read all the books - the sex manuals and the so-called marital aids - and they had filled her with a need that she just could not get Jack to fill. Sexual hunger grew inside her and sexual frustration threatened to drive her crazy. She had almost snapped during the card party when Becky started talking about how the bold black man had accosted her and had asked for sex. She had almost run from the table into the bathroom to get herself off with her fingers. She had been so lost in sexual desire that she hadn't heard Cassie the first time that Cassie reminded her that she had to leave at three to get home and let the washing machine repairman into her house. Cassie actually had to reach over and shake her shoulder to get her attention. As she pulled into her drive she wondered if she had time to use her dildo before the repairman arrived.

She was just taking the large rubber dick out of her dresser drawer when the doorbell rang. "Shit, shit, shit," she cried as she threw the rubber cock across the room. She composed herself as she headed for her front door and hoped that the repairman would be quick. She desperately needed to get herself off. She opened the front door and her eyes took in the tall Afro-American standing there tool box in hand. Her knees went weak.

"Hi. Mrs. Cleary? I'm here to look at the washing machine."

Wordlessly she stepped aside to let him in. "Ri…rig…right this way," she stammered as she led the black man to her laundry room. Thoughts and images were running wild in Karen's head. She saw herself ripping off her clothes in front of this man. She saw herself on her knees sucking his black cock. She saw herself being taken on the floor as she looked up at the huge black man looming over her. Then she noticed him looking at her with a weird expression on his face. "What's the matter?" she demanded, frightened, yet strangely turned on by the thought.

"Uh…nothing lady, nothing." He turned his attention to the washing machine as she hurried back up to her bedroom. She picked up her dildo from where she had thrown it, hurriedly stripped off her clothes and lay down on the bed. As she worked on herself with the large fake rubber cock she imagined that it was the black repairman's dick. She closed her eyes and in her mind she saw her legs clamped around his hard body, his rich chocolate skin glistening with sweat as he sought to gain his pleasure by giving her pleasure. "Oh shit," she moaned as she took the fake cock out of her pussy and dropped it on the bed. As if in a trance Karen got up from the bed and went downstairs.

The man heard her coming and he turned to face in her direction. His eyes got big as they took in the sight of her naked white body walking toward him. She read the nametag on his uniform shirt and asked in a voice fairly dripping with sex, "Do you work on anything besides washing machines Jason?"

The man was too surprised to answer. He'd heard about things like this from other repairmen, but he had never believed them. Karen saw the tent in the man's trousers. He had a hard on and she had given it to him. She walked up to him and rubbed her naked leg against the lump in his pants and even as Karen's fingers moved to Jason's zipper she couldn't believe that she was doing it. She was a loving wife - a good girl, not some slut - and she knew that she wasn't the kind of woman to do such a thing, knowingly commit adultery. This wasn't her, this was a dream, and a fantasy and she would wake up any minute now. Then she had his fly open and her feverish fingers reached inside and took hold of his hard cock.

"Fuck me," she moaned into Jason's ear.

"Right here, right now. Take me, make me your bitch."

"Hey, whoa up lady, I..." and Karen hissed at him, "Do it damn you, fuck me, fuck me hard and make me scream."

Karen was stroking his shaft and then suddenly he put both hands on her shoulders and pushed her to her knees. "You want it lady, you got it, every fucking inch of it."

He grabbed her head with both hands and shoved his boner straight into her mouth. Karen gagged. She'd only had a cock in her mouth twice before and neither of them had been half as big as the one now fucking her face. She struggled and pushed him away, "Not that," she gasped, "I want you to fuck me. I want you to fuck me hard and make me cum."

Jason reached down and with his powerful black hands he picked her up and set her down on the dryer. He pulled her legs apart and with one powerful stroke he plunged his hard cock into her pussy. As his hard cock lanced into her, Karen realized that this wasn't part of any fantasy, this was real. She panicked. She had never cheated on her husband before, this couldn't be happening to her, "No, wait, this is wrong, we can't, I'm married," she cried as she tried to push the big black man away from her. She couldn't budge him and he continued to slam his hard cock into her.

"Tough shit lady. You should have thought of all that before you unzipped me."

And then, suddenly, Karen wouldn't have stopped him even if she could have. His rough fucking of her body had started a fire in her; a level of sexual arousal she had never before experienced flowed through her body. She hadn't felt this hot in years. Karen's hands reached up and grabbed Jason's shoulders and she hissed, "Oh yes, oh God yes, fuck me, fuck me hard and make me cum."

Jason laughed. "Like this big black dick? No more this is wrong, we can't and I'm married bullshit? You just another white whore who likes black cock, ain't you?"

"Yes," Karen moaned, "I'm a white whore. Fuck me, fuck me hard."

"You love my black cock, don't you?"

"Oh God yes. I love your cock baby, just keep fucking me. Make me cum baby, make me cum."

Jason grinned as he looked down on the face of the little white housewife who was begging him for his cock and he wondered how much he could charge his buddies for some of her tight white pussy. Karen, unaware of the plans Jason was making concerning her future, was lost in the intensity of the strongest orgasm she had ever experienced. She moaned and her head whipped from side to side as she came so hard she cried. Then she felt a small degree of sanity returning and with it came the horror of what she had just done. She had just engaged in un-protected sex with a man not her husband and a black man at that. Oh sweet Jesus, what if she got pregnant? Then she realized that Jason hadn't cum yet. She shoved at him, "Get off me. Please stop and get off me."

Jason laughed at her. "No way honey. You wanted this and you just got off and now it's my turn."

"No, you can't! You can't cum in me. I'm not safe."

"Tough shit lady. You should have thought of that before you decided to act like a slut."

"Then pull out and cum on my stomach or cum on my tits or face, but please, please pull out and don't cum in me."

"Sorry honey, but I kind of like the idea of a sweet looking white bitch walking my kid to school in the morning."

Jason started pounding into her faster and harder as if insistent on getting his seed planted deep inside her. The friction of his hard cock rubbing her clit set her on fire again and she wrapped her legs around the black stud who was giving her the fuck of her life. She came and then she came again as the black man furiously fucked her. He was grunting with every stroke into Karen's hot welcoming hole and then she felt his cock start to grow in her and she knew what that meant, but lost in the mindless sex of the moment she no longer thought of an unwanted black baby; her only thoughts were to make it last, to get her one great fuck before having to return to the so-so sex she had with her husband. Jason's cock erupted like Mount St. Helens and his hot cum sprayed the inside of her pussy. His blast sent her off into one more mind numbing orgasm. When Jason's cock finally died and slipped from her cunt like a limp noodle, Karen was exhausted. Exhausted and ashamed of herself for letting a moment of weakness destroy her vows to her husband. Would she be able to hide this from Jack or would he look at her and know instantly what she had done. And what if she had gotten pregnant? Oh sweet Jesus how could she have been so stupid? She felt Jason pulling her up from the dryer and she opened her eyes to see Jason grinning down at her. "Come on sweetcheeks, we got the quickie out of the way, now let's go and do it right."

"Wha…what do you mean?"

"We're going to take it to the bedroom."

"You can't! My husband will be home soon."

"Sooner or later he's going to find out you are a whore for black cock so we might as well get it over with now."

"No! No, I am not a whore for black cock. This was a mistake, a stupid mistake and you have to leave now."

"You can say you ain't a whore honey, but what you just did on the dryer proves that you are a liar."

Jason picked her up and started for the stairs to go up to the bedroom. "No, no" Karen cried as she beat on him with her tiny fists.

Jason stopped and set her down on her feet and looked down into her eyes and grinned. "I ain't fixed your washing machine yet honey. Tell you what. We either go upstairs now or I come back around noon tomorrow to fix your machine and scratch your itch. What's it to be?"

For Karen it was a no brainer; anything to get him out of the house before Jack got home.

"Okay, tomorrow at noon. Now hurry please, please go before my husband gets home."

"Sure sweetcheeks, tomorrow at noon, and sweetcheeks? I like to fuck my ladies while they wear high heels. If you don't have any, get a pair by noon tomorrow."

As Jason left Karen's house he was smiling. He'd be back the next day alright, but he wouldn't be alone. A few massive doses of hard black cock would turn the little white housewife into his black cock-loving slut and he was looking forward to all the things he could do with her and to her. Oh yes lady, you are in for one wild ride.

Through the living room window Karen watched as Jason got in his truck and drove off. Stupid, stupid, stupid she thought, how could I have been so stupid. Not only did I cheat on my husband, but I did it with a black man and I let him cum in me. Oh shit! Maybe a quick douche and a good wash can help and she hurried up the stairs to the bathroom. Working the nozzle of the douche bag past the still tender and tingling pussy lips, she remembered how good that black cock had felt and how she'd had so many orgasms and she wondered how many more she might have had if she had let Jason carry her up the stairs to her bedroom. She closed her eyes and let her mind bring back the image of being on the dryer while that hard black cock pumped into her. It was the best fuck she'd ever had and the memory of it began to make her feel all warm and tingly. She snapped out of it. Stop that, damn you. It was wrong! It was worse than wrong! It was a despicable thing for her to have done that to her husband. Okay, so Jack wasn't a great fuck compared to Jason, but Jack was a good man and she loved him. The only thing she knew for sure was that she wasn't going to be at home when Jason came knocking on the door.

Thoroughly douched, she put the douche bag away and got into the shower. As she washed herself, the steamy hot water made her relax and when the wash rag rubbed across her pussy lips she moaned and once again remembered how full her pussy had felt as Jason had stuffed his cock in her The memory of the large black man taking her caused her pussy to clamp on her finger and she fingered herself to a small orgasm. She thought of what she would tell Jack when he came home and found that the washing machine wasn't fixed. She'd just tell him that the repairman didn't have the part he needed on his truck and he would be back tomorrow to finish the job. Then she wondered which of her many pairs of high heels Jason would like the best.

End of the 1ˢᵗ Story

-
-
-
-
-
-
-

Lexy And The Delivery Boy

-
-
-
-
-
-
-

My first wife left me for a drummer in an acid rock band and my second wife left me for an old college girlfriend. That being the way my luck usually seems to go I decided that I would never bother getting married again. So why did I marry a third time knowing that the marriage couldn't possibly last a year, two years at most? I have to blame my father for that.

From the time I was old enough to understand words my father preached responsibility. To him the mark of a man was being responsible for his actions. Break a window with a baseball? Own up to it and make restitution. Fail a math test? Admit to not studying or paying attention in class. Whatever it was, you were supposed to step to the plate and accept the responsibility of your actions. So when Alexis said she was pregnant and that I was the father all I could do was marry her. Why didn't I expect the marriage to last? Well Lexy's first husband divorced her when he caught her sucking off one of his business partners. Her second husband kicked her out when he caught her fucking his brother. Her third husband divorced her when he caught her taking my cock up her tight asshole. As promiscuous as she was why did I accept that the baby was mine? Because between the time she spent with her husband and the time she spent with me she had no time for anyone else and her husband had gotten vasectomy years before. Ergo, I'm the daddy.

I was overly optimistic when I said the marriage would be over in a year, two at most. I married Lexy when she was three months pregnant and I caught her fucking another man on our third month wedding anniversary. I'm a romantic at heart and I sent Lexy a dozen roses every month on the third which was the day we were married. I had just placed the order for the flowers and had given my credit card number when I was hit with the sudden desire to go home and make love to my sexy pregnant wife. I don't know what it was, but with each passing month Lexy got a little rounder and the rounder she got the sexier I found her to be. I just couldn't keep my hands off of her. I fucked her every night, sometimes two or three times, and I fucked her in the morning before leaving for work. I told my secretary that I was going to call on customers and then I left the office to hurry on home. The florist's delivery van was parked in front of the house when I got there so I went around to the back of the house to let myself in. As soon as the delivery person was gone I would jump out, yell "Surprise" and then chase Lexy up to the bedroom and we would spend the rest of the afternoon screwing our brains out. I was the one who was surprised. I heard it before I saw it.

"You like that hard black cock you horny bitch?"

"Oh god yes. It's so hard and so big."

"Bigger than any white cock you've ever had?"

"Oh yes baby, bigger, much bigger."

"Bigger than the cock that blew up your belly?"

"Much, much bigger baby. Oh god, like that, just like that. Push it deep baby, push it deep."

I peeked around the corner into the living room and saw a naked Lexy on her hands and knees on the couch. Her heavy tits and round belly were swaying as some black kid - that's right, a kid, he couldn't have been any older than eighteen or nineteen - fed his cock into Lexy's cunt from behind. The box of roses lay on the floor, unopened, next to the couch. On the couch Lexy moaned, "Oh yes, fuck me, fuck me hard" and the young black asshole smirked as he ranted away, "Damned fine nigger loving bitch gonna get a lot of black cock from now on. You want me back tomorrow bitch?"

"Oh god yes, please."

"Too bad you're already knocked up bitch, else this load would give you a black bun in your oven. Here it comes bitch, take it all." His cum splashing her insides must have been the touch needed to set her off because she had an orgasm. The kid pulled out of Lexy and I almost laughed out loud. His cock wasn't as big as mine and I wondered what all that "Big black cock" shit was all about. The kid dangled his limp noodle in front of Lexy's face and said, "You want some more black cock bitch? Then get over here and suck me and make me hard."

Lexy went after the kid's limp cock like her life depended on getting him hard in a hurry and she did a pretty good job of it. I hate to admit it, but there was something deeply erotic about watching Lexy's tits and belly sway as she worked on the kid's cock and it did give me a hard on. Once the kid was hard he told Lexy to lie down and he picked up her legs and put them on his shoulders. "You want it lady, you put it in."

Lexy's fingers wrapped around his joint and she pulled him into her cunt and said, "Fuck me hard baby, fuck me hard and make me cum."

The kid laughed, "God lady, you sure are one horny white bitch. You like my chocolate stick?"

"Oh yes baby, shove it in, shove it deep."

"You want more black cock sweetie? Will you be my married white whore if I see to it you get plenty of hard black cock?"

"Whatever you want baby, just don't stop."

"I'll be back tomorrow with some friends and we will give you so much black meat you'll never want to look at a white cock again. You want that?"

"Anything baby, anything just don't stop fucking me."

I watched for another five minutes or so and then I left.

The marriage was over, but I would have to wait until I had all my ducks in a row and the baby was born before I went for the divorce. That night when I got home Lexy was all gushy over the flowers and wanted to race for the bedroom. I really didn't want to, but to not have gone up with her might have raised some questions and I wanted to keep things on an even keel until I was ready to make my move. It wasn't my first sloppy seconds - I'd taken them following her third husband into her - but she seemed wetter than when I had followed him. I wondered how long the kid had stayed and how much more cum he had pumped into her. I performed that night, even though reluctantly, and I tore off my usual morning piece before leaving for work. That afternoon I saw a private detective, gave him what I knew and a key to the house and permission to enter and set up any cameras or recording devices he thought he might need. I had no idea how many I followed into Lexy that night, but she was sure loose, wet and sloppy. For the next two days I kept to my routine and fucked Lexy every night and morning.

On the third day I got the detective's report complete with photos. The kid had indeed come back the next day with two friends and they had spent three hours fucking Lexy in all three of her holes. The next day he had shown up with five guys, all black, and the detective had photos of the five men handing the kid money before they went into the house and spent six hours fucking Lexy. The third day it was nine men, seven blacks and two Mexicans, and again the kid got money from all of them before letting them fuck my wife. That night when I got home and Lexy wanted to race up the stairs I told her no.

"You are too far along now and I don't want to take a chance on hurting the baby."

"But the doctor said we would be good for another six weeks."

"Doctors have been wrong before Lexy and I'm not willing to take the chance."

I haven't touched her since that day, but she is still getting plenty of black cock every day. The kid is getting rich off of her and I expect that he will take over and be her full-time pimp when I kick her unfaithful ass out. The baby is due next week and I'll probably wait until the doctor okays Lexy to have sex before I throw her out. After all, I'm not a mean man and I wouldn't want to pitch her out until her pussy was able to make her and the delivery kid a living.

The End

Madge Gives a Gift

Betsy had been my wife's best friend all through high school and college and Madge had taken it pretty hard when Betsy had married and moved to New York. The two had kept in constant touch, but Madge had not seen Betsy in almost five years. Last Saturday Betsy had called to say that her husband Rick would be coming to town on business and she had talked him into bringing her along. Madge naturally insisted that they stay with us and for the next two days she bustled around the house getting ready for company. Madge met their flight on Monday and brought them to our house.

I've known Betsy almost as long as Madge, but we were just friends, not good friends, if you know what I mean, but I'd never met her husband until now. As we were introduced I had the distinct impression that he was sizing me up, but I put the thought out of my mind when I got a good look at Betsy. She had changed - dramatically. She'd lost a good sixty pounds and you could see evidence of a lot of time spent in a gym. She was, what some of my younger co-workers would call, a 'hard body'. Her personality had also undergone a major change. She was no longer the constantly insecure girl she used to be; that person had been replaced by a very confident, self-assured woman.

The evening was spent drinking wine, talking about old times, and in the case of Rick and I, getting to know each other. We had several mutual interests and as we discussed them I again got the feeling that I was being 'measured'. At eleven, we all hit the sack since Rick's first client meeting was at eight the next morning. We gave him Madge's car to use and Madge and Betsy planned to drop me at work and then use my car to go shopping. That night I was surprised to see Betsy waiting for me when I got off work. She told me Madge was working on dinner and so she had volunteered to pick me up.

"Actually," she said, "I'm glad it worked out this way because I needed a chance to talk to you alone. I looked at her questioningly and she went on, "In fact, you are the reason that I came on this trip with Rick."

She had my full attention now. "I need you to promise me that what I say here will go no farther - not even to Madge."

I frowned at that - Madge and I have no secrets from each other and I told Betsy that.

"If the outcome of this little talk goes the way I hope it will, I'll tell Madge everything myself. If it doesn't, then she doesn't need to know. Please?"

I considered it a moment and then I said ok.

"I want you to fuck me - while Rick watches!"

It was a damned good thing that she was driving, because had I been I would have run us right off the road and killed us both.

"You can't be serious," I said.

"Oh, but I am. Hear me out. For the last two years Rick has been after me to satisfy his favorite fantasy. He wants to watch me have sex with another man. At first I told him no, but he has constantly been after me to do it and it has finally reached a point where I have to do it or tell him to take a hike. The problem is that I love him even if he is being an asshole about this and I really don't want a divorce. When I finally told him I would do it, I told him it would only happen under certain conditions. It couldn't be anyone that we knew, it would have to be done away from home, and I would have to be comfortable with whomever we chose. I have not been able to find anyone who fits my requirements, but ever since I told Rick I would do it he's been even worse at bothering me to get it on with someone. When he told me about this trip I jumped at the chance to come with him. You are an attractive man and I've known you for years and I trust you. So I'm asking you for your help. Will you please fuck me?"

I was still shaking my head in amazement when she asked the question. "What about you not doing it with someone you know?"

"That only meant back home. If things didn't go right I didn't want to be in a position where I had to continually see the other person."

I do have to admit that this 'new and improved' Betsy was a turn on, but I was a happily (and faithful) married man. "I'm flattered that you thought of offering yourself to me, but I've never cheated on Madge before, and as delicious as you look I don't think I can start now."

Betsy smiled at me and said, "I knew you would say that. Next question - would you if Madge said it was okay?"

That was an easy one, "In a heartbeat Betsy, in a heartbeat."

<<O>>

And I would have to, but there was no way that Madge was ever going to agree to something like that. The next day was a repeat of the previous day except that both Madge and Betsy picked me up after work. I t was a quiet ride home and I thought the reason might be that Betsy had talked to Madge about what she wanted me to do. Dinner was also a subdued affair, and I was not surprised when Madge pleaded a headache and retired early. I kept our guests company for a while and then I also went to bed. I found Madge staring at the ceiling and I no sooner sat down on the bed when she said:

"Did you really tell Betsy that you would like to have sex with her if it was okay with me?"

I repeated the conversation that I'd had with Betsy and told Madge that I had told Betsy I would if she could talk Madge into it.

"But that was just because she is your best friend. I couldn't just say 'hell no!' I knew there was no way it would ever happen and I wanted to leave her with some dignity. I mean it had to be hard for her to ask me that."

It was a good five minutes before Madge spoke again, "She says she loves him and doesn't want to lose him, but she says that if things keep going the way they are the marriage is going to end in divorce. She thinks her only way out is someone like you." Several more minutes of silence. "She is my oldest and dearest friend and I want to help her save her marriage, but how can I say, "Sure - go ahead and fuck my husband. I can't."

Wisely, I kept my mouth shut.

The next morning Madge drove me to work and when we got there she shut off the engine and sat staring out the windshield. She turned to me and said, "I've decided to let you do it. Betsy will pick you up tonight and the two of you can work things out. I'll go visit my mother tonight."

I didn't need to be a rocket scientist to know the response to that.

"No way baby. The only reason that I said I would do it was because I knew there was no way in hell that you would agree. You are not going to dump this on me. If you are going to use me to save your friend's marriage then it is going to be with your complete and wholehearted support. You are damn well going to have to tell me to do it and then convince me that it is not going to have an adverse effect on our marriage. I'll see you tonight." And I got out of the car.

That night Betsy was waiting for me when I got off work. When I got in the car she handed me an envelope with my name written on the front in Madge's handwriting. I opened it and read:

Please! Do it for me.
Love,
Madge

I looked at Betsy and she smiled at me nervously. "Are you really sure you want to do this?" I asked.

"I have to," she replied.

"Okay," I said, "I guess all that's left is to work out the mechanics of it. I'm not sure that I'll be able to get it up with Rick there watching, after all, I've never done this before. I think it would be best if we started and then have him come in the room."

Betsy told me to do it anyway I wanted to just so we could get it done and she could get on with her life in a normal fashion.

Two things I learned that night - Madge didn't have a clue when it came to giving blow jobs, and that I was an exhibitionist. Betsy started us off by giving me the greatest blowjob I'd ever received - she could have made a fortune doing nothing but sucking cock. I settled into a sixty-nine with her that I enjoyed so much that I didn't really want to stop. Rick came in and took a seat and I didn't even notice him come in. When we finally broke the sixty-nine I saw him for the first time, sitting in the chair with a big smile on his face and stroking his dick and for some strange reason that inspired me. Betsy and I bounced all over that bed for over an hour. She had multiple orgasms, but I could not cum. I fucked Betsy as hard and fast as I could, but I could not get my rocks off; every time I got close I would glance over and see Rick and think to myself, "Oh no. I'm not going to cum and turn her over to you" and then

I would keep on fucking Betsy. Finally Betsy told me to stop because she had to use the bathroom. While she was gone I lay on the bed with my hard on pointing at the ceiling and wondering if it would ever go down.

Betsy came back and took some lotion from the bedside table and coated my dick with it, and then she swung over me and impaled herself on my dick. She rode me for another twenty minutes and I still hadn't cum. The whole time Rick sat in the chair and stroked his dick. As far as I could tell he was saving himself for Betsy and I think she knew it because she finally told me that she'd had enough, but that she would get me off with her mouth or hands. As she lowered her mouth to my dick, two things happened at once: Rick entered her from behind, took a dozen strokes, and then exploded in her. And Madge came out of the closet from where she had witnessed everything. She approached the bed, knelt beside Betsy, and then the two of them alternated sucking my cock. I still hadn't come and Betsy eventually abandoned the effort and she and Rick headed for their bedroom. As soon as they were gone Madge pulled me onto her and said, "Fuck me baby. God, I'm so hot, fuck me."

It only took me a dozen strokes before I emptied all the stored up cum into my wife. Later, as we lay relaxing, Madge said to me:

"That was the most erotic thing that I have ever seen. I was so hot that I almost came out of the closet to go after Rick's cock."

I looked at her with a question on my face and she read it right away, "No, I don't want him, but I do want to watch you and Betsy again."

I called in sick for the rest of the week and Betsy and I fucked up a storm with Madge watching during the day, and Rick and Madge watching at night.

Rick and Betsy's marriage lasted another eight months. He loved watching her so much that he kept pushing at her to do it again. The straw that broke the camel's back was when he brought three guys home with him one night and told her to fuck them. She refused and moved out. She's back here now, living in our spare bedroom while she looks for a place of her own, and sharing me with Madge. She has given me as a reference and I've told the last five people who have called that she is a slob, keeps a filthy house, has loud parties, and has a constant stream of men going in and out at all hours of the day and night. I'm no fool - I'm keeping her in the spare bedroom for as long as I can. And the best part? Madge doesn't mind at all.

The End

-
-
-
-
-
-
-
-

Nadine's Needs

-
-
-
-
-
-
-

She was short, plump, had big tits (40DD she said) and had long, thick black hair that hung down to her ass. But she also had something that most short chubby girls don't have - she had sex appeal! She had that certain something, an aura if you will, that just radiated from her. When she walked into a room and you saw her you got an immediate hard on, your palms got wet and your eyes never left her. The funny thing was that she never realized it.

I am the service manager of a trailer sales and repair company and I first saw Nadine when she and her husband came in looking to buy a new horse trailer. I was behind the service counter when she came in and instantly everything that I mentioned above happened. My eyes followed her everywhere as she walked through the show room. She was wearing tight jeans, tennis shoes, a tank top and her hair was done up in a thick black braid and everything about her just screamed out, "Fuck me. Please, somebody fuck me." She browsed the parts racks, looked into the two-horse bumper-pull on display on the show room floor and then left. I hated to see her leave, but I'm not sure that I could have stood her being there much longer. Right then what I wanted to do more than anything was get to the men's room and beat my meat, but the phone started ringing and I got back to work.

The next time I saw Nadine was two weeks later when she and her husband brought in their old trailer to get an estimate on its possible trade in value. Her black hair was loose and it swirled around as she again browsed the parts counters and the displays of after-market truck accessories. Hidden behind the counter she couldn't see me squeezing the hard on she had given me as my eyes followed her around the room. Finally her husband came and got her and they left. Once again I wanted nothing more than a quick trip to the bathroom to relieve myself, but once again I got busy and it had to wait. It was a good thing I was single because I would have had a hard time explaining to a wife why I spent so much time in the bathroom. Nadine came in two days later to drop off her old trailer and hook up her new one and while she didn't come in the store I watched from the window as she hooked up to her new unit. As she drove off I hoped that it wasn't the last time that I'd ever see her.

Three weeks later I was working on the computer when I heard someone come in the front door. I turned around and it was Nadine. She walked up to the service counter and I said, "Good morning. Can I help you?"

She gave me a smile that made my knees go weak and said "I've got a problem with my new trailer. I can't get my interior lights to go on."

I asked her to give me a minute to get out of the program I was in and then I followed her out to her trailer. The problem was an easy one to fix and I had it ready to go in about five minutes. She asked me how much she owed for the service and I told her nothing, that we would consider it warranty work.

"How sweet of you," she said in a voice that curled my toes and she reached in her handbag and brought out a five dollar bill, "Here, at least let me give you this for your trouble."

I politely refused it, but at the last minute I said, "I'll let you buy me a cup of coffee some day."

She grinned at me and said, "It's a date."

As she drove off the lot my eyes followed her until she was lost to sight.

It was almost six weeks before I saw her again. She had run over something on the road and had blown a tire. She had put the spare on and now she needed a new spare. I sold her the tire and had it mounted and balanced and as she was writing me the check to pay the bill she looked at her watch and said, "It's lunch time and I owe you a cup of coffee. Is there a decent place close by?"

What I really wanted to say was "Yes. My apartment is just five minutes from here" but what I actually said was "There is a Denny's just down the street." She climbed into my pick up truck and I knew that I would be sniffing the seat where she was sitting for the next year. I know, it sounds depraved, but that is the effect that Nadine had on me. On the way we made the usual small talk, nothing of any consequence, just questions about how long I'd worked at the trailer place, did I like my job, how long had she had horses, how was the new trailer working out for her, stuff like that. It wasn't until we were seated at Denny's that she asked me the question that turned my face red:

"Why do you look at me the way you do? From the first time I came into the showroom you have never taken your eyes off me."

I stammered, hemmed and hawed, and I don't think anything coherent came out of my mouth and she gave me her toe-curling grin again and said, "Don't be embarrassed, I like the way you look at me." Then her mood changed and she said, "I just wish I could get my husband to look at me that way."

Then she started telling me about how she thought he had lost interest in her, that they hardly ever made love anymore and that she thought he probably had a girl on the side. "He goes out at night, is gone for hours and when he comes back he smells like he has just had a shower and he won't tell me where he has been. The only thing I can think of is that he is getting it on with some floozy and he has to wash her stink off of him before he gets home. It's just not fair! I have so much to give and he doesn't even want it."

She saw the look on my face and she said softly, "But you do, don't you? That's the look that I see on your face every time you look at me. I'm sorry. I shouldn't have talked to you like this, but you seemed so nice and I needed someone nice to talk to."

I 'aw shucked' it and lunch was pretty silent after that. When the check came she reached for it, but I grabbed it, "You were going to buy me coffee," I said, "not lunch. This way you still owe me a coffee and maybe I'll get a chance to see you again."

The ride back to work was as silent as lunch had been and when we got there she got out of my truck and headed for hers. Half way to it she turned and came back. She handed me a piece of paper and said, "Call me. Tonight. Any time after six." Then she turned and left.

The rest of the day I couldn't do anything right because my mind was not on my job, it was on that little piece of paper in my pocket. I kept taking it out and looking at it - even her handwriting was sexy. Damn Lord, why me?

I got off work at five and was home by five-ten. I sat and stared at the phone for the next fifty minutes while my mind kept churning away. Did I really need this? Why should I drive myself crazy over a woman who could never be mine? All calling her would do would be to prolong the agony. Better to just put her out of my mind and get on with my life. At six oh one I was punching in the numbers on the phone and after two rings her throaty, sexy voice said, "Hello?"

I was tongue-tied; I couldn't say anything and I was about to hang up when she said, "I wondered if you would call. I'm making a pot of coffee. Would you like to come over and get the cup I promised you?"

I stood there with the phone to my ear, struck dumb by the invitation and she said, "It's alright really. Tonight is one of my husband's nights out and I could really use some company. A friendly face that I could talk to."

Against my better judgment I asked for directions. It took me a half an hour to get there and when I pulled in to her drive I could understand how she could feel alone. Her place was six hundred acres just off County 21 and I hadn't seen another house for five miles. She met me at the door and led me into the kitchen and poured me a cup of coffee and we sat at the kitchen table and talked. Mostly she talked and I listened. She pretty much told me her life story, how she and her husband had been childhood sweethearts, had married just out of high school and what their hopes and dreams had been. And suddenly it was ten o'clock and she looked at me and said, "Listen to me babble on. You just sat there and listened and I didn't even give you a chance to say a word. Next time you do the talking and I'll listen. There will be a next time, won't there? Please don't say no. I need someone I can talk to."

How was I going to say no? She walked me to the door and just before I left she stood on tiptoes and kissed me on the cheek. "Thank you for being a friend. He goes out again day after tomorrow. Come have coffee with me again?"

Again, how could I refuse? On the drive home I wondered why I had let myself get into the position I was in; all of a sudden I was the shoulder to cry on, the friend to listen to all of her woes and I had no one to blame but myself.

<<O>>

Wednesday Nadine called me at two in the afternoon, "You are coming over tonight, aren't you?"

I wanted to say no and put an end to driving myself crazy, but I said yes and she said she would have the coffee ready when I got there. She met me at the door and sat me down at the kitchen table and poured me a cup of coffee. "Be right back." And she left the room. I added cream and sugar to the cup and was looking down at the cup and stirring it when I heard her say, "Do you think my tits are too big?" and I looked up to set her standing naked in the doorway. "Most guys seem to like looking at them. I don't know why, I always thought that my legs were my best feature."

I stared at her, scarcely daring to breathe lest she turn and leave. She was the goddess of sex personified.

"What's the matter? Cat got your tongue?"

She walked toward me and I noticed that she did indeed have great legs and she had made them even sexier by wearing high heels. She walked up to me and knelt down and her hands went to the zipper on my trousers. She looked up at me, "I know I'm acting like a brazen whore, but I'm human and I have needs that need to be taken care of. I know you want me, but I also know that you are too nice a guy to make a move on me so I'm taking things into my own hands." And she did. She took out my already hard cock and then looked up at me again, "You aren't going to run away on me, are you?" and when I stared down at her without saying anything she gave me a little smile and said, "Of course you won't. You are too nice a guy to do that to me." Then she took me in her mouth.

I've had blowjobs before, some very good ones, but I'd never had one near as exquisite as the one Nadine gave me. She didn't just suck my cock; she made love to it. When she had me ready to cum and I tried to pull out of her mouth she wouldn't let me go. I had the strongest orgasm of my life and Nadine gulped, sucked and swallowed every last bit. When I softened she let me out of her mouth and said, "The first time is always the fastest so I like to get it out of the way. That way when you fuck me it will last longer. You are going to fuck me, aren't you?" She laughed, "Of course you will. There is no way I'm going to let you leave unless you do." She stood up and leaned forward, "Kiss me lover. Taste how Nadine tastes with you in her mouth."

It was the hottest kiss that I had ever experienced and when it was over she took me by the hand and led me into her bedroom.

<<O>>

When I got home I lay staring up at the ceiling and wondered why I'd had the rotten luck of finding the girl of my dreams only to have her be married to someone else. I could not understand how her husband could keep his hands off of her; how he could possibly want to spend time with another woman when he had Nadine at home. Nadine was the most fantastic piece of ass I'd ever had and she wanted to do it all - suck my cock, fuck me, kiss me, she even had me fuck her in the ass - and she wanted to do it all night. But of course we couldn't. Her husband usually got home at eleven-thirty so she had to get me out of the house by ten-thirty to give her a margin of safety. As I was leaving she said, "Day after tomorrow, same time?" I answered her by taking her in my arms and kissing her passionately before she pushed me out the door. The next day at noon I was surprised to see Nadine pull onto the lot. She came in and said, "Had lunch yet?" I said no and she said, "Come on then, my treat." We went outside and she said, "This time I'll drive" and as we pulled off the lot she said, "Tell me how to get to your place." I looked over at her and she smiled at me, "I said my treat lover, and you are my treat. I can't wait until tomorrow night."

I was very, very late returning from lunch. Every time I tried to get out of the bed Nadine would pull me back down and find a way to get me hard again. Before she dropped me off at work I gave her a key to my place so she could meet me there instead of at work. No sense taking a chance that her husband might find out and if Nadine and I left there too many times together it would surely be noticed.

For the next two weeks I went out to Nadine's every Monday, Wednesday, and Friday and she did her absolute best to fuck me to death. On almost every day during the week I would go home for lunch and find her naked and waiting for me on the bed. It was good times and bad times. The good times were every minute that I spent with her and the bad times were when I was alone because that's when I had to face reality - I knew that it was going to have to end.

One day, after we had finished "lunch" Nadine asked me if I would do her a favor; she wanted me to follow her husband one night and find out just where it was he was going and to see who he met. I was a little reluctant to do it, but an absolutely superb blowjob convinced me to do what she asked. That Wednesday night I was waiting at the crossroads of County 21 and Hwy 73 when my cell phone rang and Nadine told me that her husband had just left the house. A couple of minutes later his truck pulled up at the stop sign and then turned left. I gave him a thirty-second head start and then I pulled out of the Texaco station and followed. Fifteen minutes later he pulled into the parking lot of Barron's Roadhouse and went inside. I got out of my truck and followed him in, but once inside I couldn't see him anywhere so I sat down at the end of the bar and ordered a beer.

About five minutes later Nadine's husband came out of the back room tying on an apron as he walked behind the bar. He walked up to the bartender, who was just setting my beer down in front of me, and said, "Okay Sid, your relief is here."

The bartender looked at his watch and said, "You're half an hour early."

Nadine's husband (his name was Dale) said, "I know, but I can use the extra time."

Sid said, "How close are you to being able to buy your wife that horse?" and Dale said that six more weeks should do it. Sid asked him if he was going to quit then and Dale said, "Well, I like it here and I like the people that work here and I like most of the regular customers, but I'd really rather be home with Nadine. As soon as I surprise her with the horse on her birthday I'm out of here."

Well, there it was. The end that I'd always known was coming. I finished my beer and left. On the way back to Nadine's I flirted with the idea of telling her that Dale had met a buxom blonde named Wanda or something. I would buy me six more weeks, but in the end I knew I couldn't do it. Nadine would eventually find out that I had lied to her and I didn't want that to happen. If she ever came in for service on her trailer I wanted her to be able to smile warmly at me. When I got to her place I told her what I had found out and I saw her face change, whether it was sadness over the fact that she had misjudged her husband or contempt for herself for cheating on him, I didn't know. I said, "I'm sorry Nadine." And I turned to go. Just as I reached the door she said, "And just where do you think you are going?"

I turned to her and said, "Well, now that you know he's not

cheating on you I thought you'd want me to go."

She smiled, "Nothing's changed baby. He's not here and you are and Nadine needs a cock to play with."

After it was over she gave me the first soft, tender kiss that she'd ever given me and said, "I always said you were a nice guy, but I have a confession to make and when I'm done you may not think I'm very nice. I lied to you when I said that Dale doesn't fuck me anymore. He fucks me damned near every night. I took up with you because I thought he was cheating on me and I wasn't going to let him get away with it. If cheating was good enough for him, then it would be good enough for me. I picked you because I wanted a nice guy, someone who would treat me nice and not like some whore stepping out on her husband and I've grown fond of you and I have no intention of letting you go. You have turned me into your slut and I like it and I'm not going to stop. It will be harder to do when he quits his part time job, but at the very least we will still have our lunch hours. Face it baby, Nadine needs you and she ain't going to let you go. Now, fuck me one more time before you have to leave."

That was three years ago and Nadine and I still get together every chance we get. She loves Dale and has no intention of ever leaving him. He is crazy about her and wouldn't let her go anyway, at least not unless he becomes terminally stupid. As for me, I take what I can get whenever I can get it and at the very least I get to go to bed every night knowing that Nadine needs me.

The End

-
-
-
-
-
-
-

Old Jared Knows

-
-
-
-
-
-
-

There I stood in hospital greens, video camera in hand, ready to tape the birth of our first child. The doctor, the head nurse, the rest of the delivery room crew moved around in their well-practiced ballet. Janet was breathing hard and moaning as the doctor was telling her to concentrate, to push, and the nurses were all cooing, "Everything is going to be okay honey" and other comforting things. Then someone said, "Here it comes." And I zoomed in with the telephoto lens. We had wanted the surprise so when the ultrasound was done we told them not to tell us the sex of the baby, "We want it to be a surprise" and a surprise it was - a very big surprise. As the baby came out into its first day of life in the open air everyone there saw that the skin of the baby was not white.

I went home from the hospital not understanding what had just happened. How could my wife have delivered a black baby? I mean the answer was obvious, but I was too shocked to be thinking straight and it wasn't until after I got home and had several stiff drinks that I faced up to the fact that my wife had been impregnated by a Negro. The child that I had joyously awaited since the day that Janet told me she was pregnant was not mine. The father was a black man. My wife had been fucking a black man! I don't know what killed me more; the fact that the hoped for child wasn't mine or that my wife was an unfaithful whore.

I'd left the hospital right after my 'big surprise' and I hadn't yet faced Janet. I had no idea what she was going to say or if I was even going to go back to the hospital and listen. I didn't even know if I was going to the hospital and bring her home when the doctor released her or just let her fend for herself. Maybe I should just let her call her black lover and let him pick her up and take her home with him. God knows there wasn't much left at our apartment for either of us to come home to. I couldn't stay there. There would be too many painful memories associated with the place. I thought that maybe the best thing to do was quickly move out while Janet was in the hospital and just never see her again. I couldn't understand it. I'd thought we'd been so happy together. How could she have done this to me, to us?

In the end the need to know was stronger than the outrage I felt and I went back to the hospital. Janet was in a semi-private room and there was someone occupying the other bed. I was extremely angry, but I'm the type who hates public scenes so all I could do was stand there and stare at Janet. At first she wouldn't look at me and she kept her face turned away from me. Then she said something, but it was in a voice so low that I couldn't hear. I leaned down and said, "I didn't hear that."

"You saw the baby?"

"Yes."

"So you know."

"Yes, unfortunately I know."

"I'm sorry. It wasn't supposed to happen, I'm sorry."

"What wasn't supposed to happen?"

"They weren't supposed to get me pregnant."

They? They weren't supposed to get her pregnant? Sweet Jesus, what had she been doing while I sat around fat, dumb, happy and secure in our love for each other? Just then the doctor came in and read her chart and then told her he was going to release her in the morning. He left and then Janet said again, "I'm sorry Billy, I didn't mean for this to happen. I love you Billy, I really do."

"Yeah, well that doesn't help any Janet, not one little bit. Best you get on the phone and call your black lover and let him know to come get you and take you home tomorrow."

I turned and walked out of the room as she cried out, "Billy, please Billy…"

The next morning the phone rang and it was Janet. "Please Billy, come and get me. There isn't anyone else I can call. Please Billy."

The ride home was a silent one. Janet apparently afraid to speak and I, for some strange reason, not wanting to say anything while the baby was with us. Once in the house I left Janet to take care of her kid and I went into the kitchen to make myself a stiff drink and then I sat down at the table to wait for her to come in and face me. I was on my second drink and she still hadn't appeared so I hollered out, "Janet, get in here and let's get this over with."

"I'm on the couch. I don't want to sit on those hard chairs. I'm sore and I need to sit on soft cushions."

Her tone of voice was the first indication that the unfaithful slut didn't intend to be all that contrite. I built myself another drink and went into the living room and sat down across from her. She opened the ball, "I suppose you will be leaving me?"

"What did you expect? Did you think you were going to hand

me a black baby and that I was going to go, "Ooh, isn't she just so precious" and then we would live happily ever after?"

"No, no I didn't think that, but I did have some hope that our love for each other would have been strong enough that we could at least try and work through this."

"Love? You hit me with a black kid and tell me that you are gangbanging blacks and you expect that I'm still going to love you?"

"It wasn't the way you make it sound."

"Oh no? The baby speaks for itself Janet, and as far as the gangbanging goes you told me that yourself. You are the one who said, "They weren't supposed to get me pregnant". "They" means more than one Janet and in my book more than one is a gang fuck."

"Damn it Billy, that's not the way it was. Okay, there was more than one, a lot more, but you make it sound like I was going out and picking them up and that's not what happened. I love you Billy and I would never have run around on you. I would never have gone out looking for another man, never. When you get right down to it what happened to me is all your fault. If it hadn't been for you it never would have happened."

"My fault? That's a laugh. I can understand your trying to put the best face on what you did, but my fault?"

"Yes Billy, your fault. You are the one who set the whole thing up, you and your damned penchant for phone sex when you are away from home. You are the one who has me stay at the office late when you are out of town so you can call the 800 number and have phone sex. You are the one who was so cheap that you didn't want to run up our home phone bill. If I had been at home it never would have happened."

"And just how does our having phone sex put black cocks into you?"

"It happened the week of Thanksgiving. You left on your business trip Monday and told me to be in the office waiting for your call at eight that night. I was there and I took the call the way I always did. My skirt and underpants were off and I had my rubber cock and I was lying on my desk with my legs spread. While we talked I worked on myself with the dildo and I came the same way I always did and the same as always I laid there in the warm glow that I always experience after an orgasm. You had already hung up and I was laying there all warm and fuzzy feeling and stroking my clit with my fingers when I heard, "That's not right, you having to do that. Old Jared knows what you need pretty lady."

"I looked up and saw one of the men from the janitorial service standing there and looking down at me and he had his cock out and was stroking it. Try and understand Billy. He wasn't ten feet across the room standing in the doorway where I would have had time to get up - he was standing right there! I had been lying there, eyes closed, basking in the afterglow of my orgasm. My feet were flat on the desk, my legs were spread wide and my pussy was wet from our phone sex and all he had to do was take a half step forward and push and he was in me. He grabbed my legs and held me and there was nothing that I could do. I tried to pull away, I screamed at him to stop, but I was pinned to the desk. I could bend at the waist, but I couldn't get upright enough to even beat at him with my fists. He just held my legs and smiled down at me and talked to me.

"Don't fight it missy, old Jared knows how to give you what you need. Been a long time since I had any white pussy. Don't you worry none baby girl, old Jared will treat you right."

"All I could do Billy was lie there and take it and you know me Billy, you know how much I love sex. I hadn't even come all the way down from the orgasm you gave me over the phone and there I was being fucked by an old black man. My body responded Billy. I'm sorry, but the more that old man fucked me the more I got into it and it wasn't long before I was begging him to make me cum. And then he took one of those walky-talky things off his belt and said something into it and a couple of minutes later two more men came into the room. By then I was screaming at that old man to get me off. I felt him shoot into me and I was so close and I cried for him not to stop, to get me off, but he just chuckled and said, "Old Jared said he'd take care of you baby girl and he has." He stepped away from me and one of the others took his place. They never did let me come down Billy. They took me one after the other until I passed out from exhaustion. I came so many times Billy that they actually caused me to pass out."

"Why did you even do the sex talk with me if there were other people in the building?"

"I didn't know that they were there. The cleaning crew always comes in after midnight, but because of the holiday they had changed their schedule. I had no idea I wasn't alone in the building."

"Why didn't you call the police when it was over?"

"I couldn't call the police."

"Why not?"

"Because they had me on tape."

"So? It is still rape. Just because they were dumb enough to tape themselves raping you shouldn't have kept you from calling the cops. Shit Janet, the tape was the proof."

"Yeah Billy, proof that I was a cock hungry slut. I'm on tape begging a bunch of black guys to fuck me."

"Am I missing something here? Why would a bunch of janitors be carrying around a video camera?"

"They didn't tape me at work. They taped me at Jared's apartment. When I passed out they picked me up and took me from the office to his apartment. When I woke up I was naked on his bed and he was fucking me and there were a bunch of guys there cheering him on and telling him to hurry up so that they could be next. They didn't let me off that bed until noon on Tuesday. They fed me lunch and then took me right back to bed. They didn't let me go until Wednesday morning and by then I could barely walk. You came home horny that night and I told you we couldn't make love because I was sick and then I had to pretend I was sick for the next four days to give my pussy enough time to tighten up before I could have sex with you."

"Three guys fucked you steady for a day and a half?"

"No Billy, not three. I don't have a clue how many fucked me. All I know is that Jared had a lot of friends; an awful lot of friends."

"Why didn't you tell me? We could have gotten an abortion."

"Two reasons Billy. One, I thought that the baby was yours. I was on the pill the night all of this happened. A week later I ran out of pills and went four days before I got my refill and you made love to me on three of those nights and so I did really think that the baby was ours."

"You said two reasons."

"Yes I did, didn't I?"

Janet looked away from me and then said, "I kind of liked it Billy. Not the part at Jared's apartment, but when the three of them were taking me on my desk I had orgasm after orgasm."

"So you did it again?"

"Yes."

"When?"

"Every time you went out of town I had to call Jared and let him know when we were going to have phone sex."

"You had to call him?"

"He threatened to make the tape public if I didn't and I couldn't let you see that tape Billy. I just could not let you see the slut I was for all those blacks. I couldn't let you see me screaming for joy while I had a cock in my ass, my pussy and my mouth at the same time."

"Was it just Jared?"

"No Billy, it was Jared, Dolman and Sam, the other janitors."

"Why did it have to be when I called?"

"Because they got a charge out of fucking me while you were having phone sex with me."

"All those moans and cries weren't caused by your dildo?"

"No Billy, I had a cock in me every time we talked."

"Maybe that's when you got pregnant?" "No Billy. The next time I was with them I was on my pills, I had a diaphragm and I used spermicide."

"They even fucked you when you were pregnant?

"Right up until two weeks ago. Can I ask you something Billy?"

"What?"

"Does it turn you on hearing about it and thinking about all those black cocks pounding into me?"

"Of course not!"

"Then why do you have a large tent in your pants?" I looked down and saw that she was right.

"I'll bet that my talking about my black lovers did that to you. I can't fuck you Billy, but if you want I'll suck you off."

I wouldn't have believed it of myself, but listening to her tell me about her three black lovers and what they did while I was on the phone with her gave me a hard on every time she did it. It is kind of hard to toss out someone who keeps your dick hard and then sucks you off so Janet and I are still together. We've told everyone that Samantha is adopted, but no one believes it. Hell, why should they? They all knew Janet was pregnant. I still call Janet when I am out of town and every time I'm talking to her I have the image of three black men fucking her silly while we talk and I end up beating myself raw. Last week the doctor cleared Janet to have sex again and I spent all weekend buried in her while she described what her black lovers did to her. Yesterday I flew to Kansas City and tonight I called home and started having phone sex with her. After about five minutes of listening to her moan and groan I thought I detected something in the background. "Janet, is someone there?"

"Yes baby, Jared is here."

"At the house?"

"Yes baby."

"Is he fucking you?"

"Yes baby, his cock is buried in me and Sam and Dolman are waiting their turn."

"Why?"

"I had to call him baby. I told you that I have to call him when you are out of town and plan on having phone sex. If I didn't he might show the tape around and we don't want that, do we?"

I heard a voice say, "He knows we are here?" Janet moaned and said yes. "Give me the phone." There was a pause and then, "Don't you worry none now, old Jared gonna take real good care of this white lady."

"Put her back on."

A pause and then, "Yes baby?"

"You tell him he better start wearing condoms or I'm going to start asking for child support. Oh, and Janet?"

"Yes baby?"

"Tell him I want a copy of that tape. Now, where were we?"

"You were telling me how hard you were going to fuck my ass and then oh,oh, oh god, yes baby, like that, hard, harder, fuck me, fuck me, make me cum, yes baby, hard, like that, oh, oh, oooooohhhhh." And I blew my load all over the motel room floor as I listened to her orgasm over the phone.

The End

-
-
-
-
-
-
-
-

Patty Ann, Brad and Me

-
-
-
-
-
-
-

I watched her dress for the party and thought for the thousandth time how fortunate I had been to have her say yes when I asked her to marry me.

As I watched her I knew that the party was going to be special. She was going all out to showcase what she had. Black lacy shelf bra that lifted her breasts so the low cut blouse could display the creamy upper slopes and the enticing cleavage. An almost non-existent black thong that I had never seen before. Her long tanned legs were stockingless as she put on a pair of strappy sandals with four inch heels. She stepped into a short black skirt that came down to mid-thigh and displayed her legs to the fullest. As a finishing touch she put an ankle chain on her right ankle and a gold chain with a locket around her neck. Still more things I'd never seen before. She spun around in front of me and asked:

"How do I look?"

"Good enough to eat."

"Good. That's the look I am going for. Come on; we don't want to be late."

As she headed for the bedroom door I rolled her comment over in my mind.

"That's the look I am going for."

Too bad the look wasn't for me.

I met Patricia Ann Cummings on our first day at Longview High School. I had gone to middle school on the north side of the county and Patty had attended middle school on the south side. We ended up sitting next to each other in that first day's first class and I was smitten. I thought that she was the loveliest thing I'd ever seen and before the day was over I asked her if she would like to go the movies with me. She said she would love to and that date led to a second which led to a third and then a fourth. We dated for a couple of months and then I asked her to go steady with me and she said no. She said she really liked me a lot, but that there were a lot of other boys that she thought were cute and that she might like to go out with.

For the next two years I asked her out at least once a week and maybe one time in four she would say yes. I thought since she kept saying yes to me that I would sooner or later have the inside track with her. That all changed in the twelfth grade. One day I asked her out and she told me that she wouldn't be able to date me anymore because she was going steady with Brad Metzler.

Through senior year I dated a couple of other girls, but my heart wasn't really in it. I would end up comparing them to Patty Ann and they never measured up. I didn't even go to the senior prom because I couldn't bear to see Patty in Brad's arms as they danced.

Patty was still friendly with me and would sit with me at lunch from time to time in the school cafeteria. We would talk about things going on with our classmates, what we were going to do when we went to college and the like. I was pretty good in math, but Patty was only so so and she would occasionally ask if she could study with me and I of course never said no.

She and Brad got into an argument about mid-way through our senior year and they broke up. I moved in and for about a month Patty and I were a couple and then one day I asked her what she wanted to do on the coming weekend and she told me that she was going to a party with Brad. From then on they were back together. Graduation came and Patty and Brad took off on a trip with Brad's parents and I didn't see them again until the fall.

It was, in the immortal words of Yogi Berra, "de-ja vu all over again." It was the first day of class at the local college and I was sitting in the auditorium waiting for freshman indoctrination to begin when someone sat down in the seat next to me. I looked over and saw that it was Patty Ann. I looked around and didn't see Brad and Patty read my mind.

"He won't be here until next week. He had something that he had to do with his father."

"Since he isn't around would this be a good time to ask you to go to Jane's party with me Friday night?"

"Why do you keep trying Rob? You know I'm Brad's girl."

"A guy can only hope."

"But why?"

"I can't tell you, but I like to think that if I hang in there it will someday be to my benefit."

"What do you mean you can't tell me why? Does that mean you don't know yourself or is it something that you don't think you can tell me?"

"Let's just say that I know when to keep my mouth shut."

"Okay then, be that way. But Brad will be back in time to take me to the party so no, I can't go with you."

"At least save me a dance."

"We'll see."

As we sat there and listened to the parade of people telling us what to expect, what not to expect and explaining the rules and regulations that would govern our lives for the next four years I thought about Patty and her question - "Is it something that you don't think you can tell me?" That was it in a nutshell. I knew better than to bad mouth Brad to her, but the plain and simple fact was that Brad was an asshole and sooner or later he was going to hurt her. I couldn't tell her that because she wouldn't believe me and all it would accomplish is that I would poison her against me. All I could do was hang around and hope to be there to help pick up the pieces when the time came.

I wanted Patty, but I finally accepted that I might never get her so I started dating and stopped trying to compare my dates to Patty. I dated half a dozen, necked with most of them, but it wasn't until I met Bonnie that I found one I wanted to date often. She was a hot kisser and liked grinding her body into mine when we danced.

It was our third date and we were necking hot and heavy in front of her dorm. We had been to a party and had done some dirty dancing and I mean some "real get down and dirty dancing" and I had a very hard and aching cock and the necking wasn't making things easier. I needed to get home to the privacy of my bedroom and take care of it. Suddenly Bonnie broke the kiss and said:

"I'll suck your dick if you will eat my pussy."

The look on my face must have been priceless. Bonnie said, "What? You've never had your dick sucked before?"

The fact of the matter was that I hadn't. I was a stone assed virgin, but I wasn't going to tell Bonnie that so what I did say was:

"I've never eaten a pussy. I don't know how."

Bonnie broke out in a big smile and said, "Oh goody! I get to be your first and I get to teach you to do it the way I like. Have you got enough to spring for a motel room?"

That night opened my eyes. I could have cried over all the times I never even tried to do things with other girls because I was so hung up on Patty. As soon as we were in the hotel room Bonnie said:

"Come here lover so I can unwrap my present." And then she undressed me. When she had me naked I returned the favor and I think by the way I fumbled with her bra hooks she got an idea of just how inexperienced I was. When I had her naked she pushed me back on the bed and said:

"I'll do you first and then we can concentrate on teaching you how to make the girls want to chase after you."

How do you describe your first blow job? I can't describe mine because I was so buried in sensations that all I could think about was how totally awesome it was. I didn't want it to end, but it did and all too quickly. I spurted and Bonnie kept sucking until I went soft.

"First blow job?" Bonnie asked and I sheepishly nodded yes. "The right way to do it is that you are supposed to tell the girl when you are ready to cum. Not all of us like to swallow. Be honest with me sweetie; you are a virgin aren't you?"

Again I sheepishly nodded a yes.

"Nothing to be ashamed of sweetie; we all have to have a first time. I love it that I get to be yours."

We didn't leave that motel room until seven the next morning and by the time the motel door closed behind me I knew how to eat pussy the way that Bonnie liked having it done, I knew I loved blow jobs (and pussy); I found out how much fun a sixty-nine could be and I had lost my virginity three times over. As we dressed Bonnie said:

"Next time we will do some anal."

"Then there will be a next time?"

"Oh yes sweetie, most definitely yes. I still have a ton to teach you."

I can't say that Bonnie and I became a couple because we didn't. Bonnie still dated other guys and I wasn't silly enough to believe that I was the only guy she had sex with, but she still managed to fit me in (no pun intended) two or three times a week. So she was seeing other guys, so what? I was still having more fun that the law should allow. And Bonnie did make me feel like a stud because a lot of times she would call me and ask me if I was up (again, no pun intended) for a night with her.

<<O>>

I would occasionally run across Patty and Brad at parties and dances and I began to notice something. If I was alone or with some girl other than Bonnie, Patty always seemed to have a smile for me, but if I was with Bonnie, Patty would look away when I caught her eye. I couldn't for the life of me figure out where Patty might have known Bonnie from or what Bonnie could have done to piss off Patty. I just filed it away as one of those questions that you would never know the answer to.

I found out that certain girls talk as much about guys as guys talk about girls. I couldn't begin to count the number of times that some guy I know bragged about how he and _____(fill in the blank) had fucked all night and what a great cock sucker she was. Girls must do the same. I was at a party one night and I had come stag. While I was there Sue Wilson came up to me and said:

"Bonnie says you are a fun date. Why don't you give me a call sometime?"

The next time I saw Bonnie I asked her about it.

"Why that little whore! I thought the bitch was my friend and now she's trying to cut in on my action."

"Cut in on your action?"

"I told the slut how good you were at eating pussy and I guess she wants to try you out to see if I know what I'm talking about."

"And just how many others did you share that little tidbit with?"

"Don't go getting all pissy with me over this baby. I won't be around forever and when I'm gone there will be a good half dozen girls who are going to try and get you to ask them out."

I did start paying attention to the girls that Bonnie seemed to spend time with and on nights I wanted to go out but Bonnie said she was busy I started calling a few of them and I did surprisingly well. Anyway, Bonnie and her friends set the stage for my next meaningful encounter with Patty Ann.

I was with Bonnie at a party and we were on the dance floor and dancing pretty close to each other when Patty and Brad came in. I caught Patty's eye and she gave me what I can only call a look of pure disgust. "What's up with that?" I wondered and then forgot about it. About an hour into the party I was at the make-shift bar making myself a drink and watching Bonnie 'dirty dance' with some guy when Patty came up to me.

"May I ask you a very personal question?"

"I think we know each other well enough for that."

"Why are you with that tramp?"

"Tramp?"

"Oh come on Rob; she is intimately acquainted with the back seats of at least half of the guys here at this party."

"And your point?"

She gave me that look of disgust again and turned and walked away. Five minutes later Bonnie came up to me and said:

"I saw you talking to Patty. What did she want?"

"Nothing. Just saying hello."

"She wants you."

I laughed at that. "She wants me? That's a crock. I've been trying to give myself to her since the ninth grade and she won't have me."

"I don't know why you haven't connected, but trust me on this - she wants you. A girl can tell about these things."

I just shook my head, took her hand and led her out onto the dance floor.

The following Monday I was sitting in the student cafeteria picking at a chicken-pot-pie and reviewing my notes for Business Law when Patty sat down across from me.

"I want to apologize, Rob. I was out of line the other night. I had no business sticking my nose into your personal life."

"So why did you?"

"I care about you Rob and I hated seeing you throw your life away on that piece of trash and her girlfriends. You deserve better Rob."

"Better wouldn't have me Patty Ann. God knows I've tried."

She looked at me blankly for a couple of seconds until she realized what it was that I had really just said.

"You don't give up do you?"

"I'm not dead yet."

"What am I going to do with you Rob; you know that I'm spoken for."

"It isn't over until I see the wedding rings on your finger Patty and even then I'll probably be around somewhere."

She shrugged her shoulders and apologized again and as she got up to leave I thought about what Bonnie had said:

"She wants you."

If Bonnie was right Patty Ann hid it well.

Summer vacation was both good and bad for me. The good part was that I had landed an internship at a local company and I was doing well and getting good reviews. The bad part was that my maternal grandparents died in an auto accident. I had been very close to Grandma Ruth and Grandpa Harry and their deaths shook me terribly.

I received a registered letter from their attorney requesting my presence at the reading of their will and that is when I found out for the first time that they had set up a trust fund for me when I was born. I would get the entire amount when I turned twenty-five. One of the provisions was that once I turned eighteen, if I went to college, I could draw against the trust for up to ten thousand a year for educational expenses. My parents had never told me about that since they had set up my college fund when I was still young. My grandparents also left me a cash bequest of twenty thousand. It bothered me that I never knew about the trust and was never able to properly thank them.

I used part of the twenty thousand to set me up in an off campus apartment, but other than that sophomore year was more of the same. I still saw Bonnie two or three times a week and when I wasn't seeing her I could usually be seen with one of the girls that Bonnie had talked me up to. Life was good, but every once in a while I would be brought down in the dumps when I'd see Patty Ann with Brad. Patty and I would run across each other every once in a while and we would talk. Always light, general conversation. She never mentioned my "tramp" and I never asked about Brad.

The year flew by and then we were into our junior year. Bonnie never came back to school after summer vacation so I was spending most of my time with Pauline French, one of the girls that Bonnie had told about my pussy eating prowess. I was having a good time with Pauline, but it was a 'nervous' good time. Pauline wanted a ring and she kept hinting that we really needed to start planning "our future" but the truth of the matter was that I didn't see a future with Pauline. She was a fun bed partner, but that is all she was as far as I was concerned. I suppose I should have done the right thing and told her straight out that marriage was not in the cards for us, but that might have caused her to drop me and I wasn't about to give up having sex four or five times a week.

Things bumped along until spring break. Two weeks after classes resumed I went into the student cafeteria for lunch and I saw Patty Ann sitting at a table in the back. I carried my tray over and sat down with her. Her face was tear streaked and she looked like hell. I asked her what was the matter and she said:

"My life sucks!"

"Oh come on Patty; things can't be that bad."

"Oh yes they can."

"So what is the problem? Uncle Rob is here to give you a shoulder to cry on."

"There isn't anything that you can do to help."

"Try me."

"I'm pregnant."

"So when is the big day?"

"I don't know. I haven't been to the doctor yet."

"Not that big day. When are you and Brad going to tie the knot?"

"We aren't. We had a big argument just before spring break and he took off. He didn't come back to school after the break and when I didn't hear from him I called his mother. She told me that he had moved to California to work for his uncle. I asked her how I could get in touch with him and she told me that he didn't want anything more to do with me and he didn't want her to give me his number."

"So he doesn't know?"

"I didn't know myself until I took the self test yesterday."

"Any chance it was a bad test?"

"I retook it again this morning and it was positive again."

"Well I wouldn't worry until a doctor confirms it."

"I have an appointment at three this afternoon, but I know it is only a formality. Oh God Rob, what am I going to do? This will just kill my mother. The shame of having an unwed mother for a daughter will just kill her. Hell! It will upset my entire family."

"It won't be that bad."

"Oh yes it will. My mother has harped on me for the last five or six years about going down the aisle as a virgin. I can't even remember how many times she told me that only sluts and whores have sex before marriage. Just to get her off my back I promised her I would be a virgin at my wedding. I am so screwed."

"Maybe not. Maybe there is a way out."

"How?"

"See the doctor first. No sense in going off half-cocked. Let's just make sure that we really have a problem."

"We?"

"You don't think I'd let you go through this alone do you?"

I drove her to the doctor's office and the doctor said, "Congratulations, you are going to be a mommy."

Patty kept a stiff upper lip until we were out of the doctor's office and then she broke down and sobbed into my shoulder until she was all cried out. As I drove her back to her car I told her that she needed to find some way to get in touch with Brad.

"Can I come to your place and call his mom from there? I can't go home to my mother in the shape I'm in right now."

"No problem. You can stay there as long as you need to."

She called Brad's mother and got the bad news. Brad had specifically told his mother that he did not want to hear from Patty under any circumstances. Patty told Brad's mother that she was pregnant and desperately needed to get in touch with Brad and Brad's mother said that Brad had told her that Patty might try something like that and to ignore

Patty. Patty hung up the phone and looked at the floor.

"I am cooked Rob, I am just so absolutely screwed."

I sat there looking at her and then knowing that it was stupid of me and that it could not turn out well I bit the bullet and said:

"There is a way."

"A way to what?"

"Take care of the problem of upsetting your family and giving the baby a name so that it won't be born a bastard."

"How can that happen?"

I told her and she was stunned. "No way," she said. "It can't work. It would be wrong. I love Brad and we will get back together; I know we will."

"Maybe, but that is in the future. This is the here and now and now is when you need to do something."

"How can you do it knowing how I feel about Brad?"

"I can do it because I've always felt the same way about you."

"What happens when Brad comes back?"

"We end it and he can legally adopt the child. No one will ever need to know."

She argued against it and I tried my best to convince her and fear of what her mother and the rest of her family would do finally swung her over and the next morning we flew to Vegas and were married by Elvis.

I loved Patty Ann, but I knew that our marriage was just a sham. I loved her enough to do what I was doing to help her, but I knew that she didn't love me. I knew she really liked me, but that was all and I made sure that the hotel where we spent the night had double beds. I was in one, under the covers, and I had turned the other one down for Patty and when she came out of the bathroom she saw the set-up. She looked from me to the other bed and then back to me and then she came and got into bed with me. I started to ask her if she knew what she was doing and she put a finger to my lips.

"I've thought about this ever since I agreed to your plan. You know that my heart belongs to Brad, but you are my husband now and I am your wife. Regardless of why we got married we are married and I intend that for as long as it lasts it will be a real marriage."

Her hand slipped down my body to my erect cock and as she wrapped her fingers around it she said:

"I guess the idea doesn't displease you."

<<O>>

It was a shock to both of our families to find out that we had eloped, but for the most part they got over it. Patty's parents told her that since she was married now they would no longer pay for her college and that upset her greatly as she was so set on getting her degree. I drew against my trust for the money to pay her tuition and books.

As far as marriages go it was so so. I loved Patty and she liked me so we got along fine, but the passion wasn't there. Most couples just married (or so I'd heard) made love anywhere and everywhere six and seven days a week until the novelty wore off, but I was getting less sex married than I was getting when I was single. Patty and I made love twice a week and I honestly believed that it was only because she thought it was her duty as a wife. But even though I seemed to be coming out on the short end I considered it the price I had to pay to have Patty.

We lived the life of married students and things seemed smooth enough. We had been married four months when I got a call from Patty's mother. Patty had been by to visit and had tripped and fallen down some stairs. She had started bleeding and they had rushed her to the hospital and Patty was in the emergency room. I hurried to the hospital and when I got there I found out that the fall had caused a miscarriage.

A few weeks after Patty had come home and recovered I sat down with her and asked her if she wanted the divorce then or wanted to wait until after graduation.

"What divorce Rob? Are you tired of me already?"

"We only got married because you were pregnant and Brad wasn't available."

"Yes we did, but we are married and I see no reason to change things."

She took me by the hand and led me to the bedroom and for the first time since Elvis joined us in holy matrimony Patty reduced me to a quivering ruin. Nothing was said by either of us, but our marriage changed that night. It was gradual at first. Our love making went to a couple of times a night on our two nights a week. Then it was three times a week. Then four. Patty Ann was more attentive and seemed to want to snuggle and cuddle more than she had in the past and our marriage started to look like the marriage that some of our friends had.

Graduation came and Patty and I found jobs and started out on our careers and while things seemed to be good I still felt a little ill at ease. I was looking over my shoulder knowing that it would all come to an end as soon as Brad came back. But Brad didn't come back and Patty never mentioned him so I gradually forgot about him.

I made arrangements to take Patty out to celebrate our first anniversary. It was on a Friday and I rushed home from work so I could change and be ready to go on time for our reservations at Duke's Steak House. I walked into the apartment and found Patty waiting for me in nothing but a pair of high heels.

"I took the liberty of cancelling our dinner reservations. I have my own idea of how we should celebrate our anniversary."

It was a long night and when she finally couldn't get me to respond any more she snuggled in next to me and said:

"Thank you for being mine."

I put my arm around her, pulled her close and prayed that I could keep on being hers.

We had been married a little over eighteen months when we tired of apartment living and went house hunting. We found a very nice three bedroom with an in ground pool and made an offer. It was accepted and we moved in. The next three years flew by and I honestly believe that there wasn't anyone in the world who could possibly be happier than I was.

And then my world turned to shit!

Patty worked for the state and got a shit load of days off during the year. Martin Luther King Day, Veteran's Day, President's Day and Columbus day were just a few of them. I only got the regular six plus my birthday so Patty had a lot of time off that I couldn't share with her. It was Columbus Day and Patty was off.

I left work early so I could go home and spend some time with her and maybe take her out to dinner. When I got home there was an unfamiliar car in the driveway and I wondered who Patty's visitor was. I called out, "Honey, I'm home" when I came in through the door, but I got no answer. I walked into the kitchen to get a Coke from the ice box and through the kitchen window I saw Patty sitting in a chair next to the pool talking to a man sitting in another chair.

The man was Brad!

They were both fully dressed and they were sitting across from each other and not close so I didn't think they had been up to anything, but human nature being what it is I went upstairs and checked the bedrooms and the dirty clothes hamper in the master bedroom. I even checked the laundry room, but found no sign that anything untoward had happened in the house. But I was not due home for another four hours and maybe Brad had just arrived and they just had not got around to doing anything yet. Who knew what might happen in those four hours.

I went outside and moved my car down the block and then went back into the house. The two of them were still sitting beside the pool so I went to the upstairs bedroom that overlooked the pool and settled in to watch.

They talked for another half hour and I noticed that Patty smiled and laughed a lot and then Brad said something that made Patty frown and cast a quick glance toward the house. She shook her head no and Brad said something else and Patty again shook her head no. Brad said something else and then they both stood up and headed for the house. I moved to the bedroom door and opened it a crack and put my ear to it.

"….tomorow for sure?" I heard Brad say and then I heard Patty say, "Tomorrow."

I thought I heard the sound of a kiss, but it could very well have been my imagination, and then the front door opened and then closed and I heard Patty humming to herself as she moved back through the house. I heard the patio door slide open and I moved back to the window and looked out. Patty was picking up the glasses that she and Brad had been drinking out of and while she was out by the pool I got out of the house. I drove to the public library and tried to kill time until it was my regular time to go home.

I pulled the day's paper from the rack and sat there trying to read it, but I couldn't concentrate. My mind was full of questions that I had no answers for. How long had Brad been back in town? How long had

Patty known it? Why hadn't she mentioned it to me? Did he just stop by the house and knock on the door? If so how did he know Patty had the day off? If he knew she had the day off how did he know she would be at home? The alternative to that was that he was invited over. If so why during the day when I wouldn't be there? And then back to an earlier question. If invited meant Patty knew he was back so why hadn't she mentioned it to me? She knew that I would find out sooner or later so why hide it from me? And what was the "Tomorrow for sure" all about? Would Patty mention that he was at the house when I got home? And the biggie:

Was my worst fear, that I would eventually lose Patty back to Brad about to be realized?

I tried to act normal when I got home and I guess I was successful because Patty didn't seem to notice any change in me. I did get the answer to one of my questions though. I asked her how her day off had been and if she had done anything with her free time.

"No baby, just a lazy day for me. I lay by the pool, read a book and worked on my tan."

We made love once that night and then I tried, with only limited success, to get some sleep.

<<O>>

I stopped at an IHOP when I left the house and called work. I told them that I was sick and wouldn't be in. I was parked where I could see that both the door to patty's office and her car in the parking lot when her lunch hour came around. At five to twelve the car that had been in my driveway the previous day pulled up outside Patty's office and parked at the curb. I could see that the driver was Brad. Patty came out, got in the car and they drove off. I didn't bother to follow them because it didn't matter. I already knew all I needed to know.

Brad was back and Patty was seeing him and hiding it from me. The handwriting was on the wall. Brad was not the distant memory that I hoped he would be and it was obvious that Patty had not put him out of her mind. Regardless of my feelings for Patty it was understood when we married that I would step aside when Brad came back. I had hoped that it would never happen, but I told her then that I understood and now

I was going to have to honor my agreement. The only question left was when she was going to drop the bomb on me.

Nothing was mentioned that night about her seeing Brad that afternoon, but when we went to bed that night Patty was insatiable and she sucked and fucked me into exhaustion. I couldn't help but wonder if it wasn't out of guilt for what she had done that day.

The next three weeks were hell on me. Patty had always stopped after work to have a drink with her co-workers, but it was usually only about once every two weeks or so. Suddenly she was stopping with them twice a week. I could count on the thumbs of one hand the number of Mary Kay, Tupperware and Avon parties that Patty had attended over the past three years, but she had gone to two of them since I first saw her with Brad out by the pool.

I knew what was going on and I finally couldn't take it anymore and I made the decision to confront Patty and get it over with. I was all set to do it after dinner, but then Patty took it out of my hands.

"Don't make any plans for Friday night."

"Why? What's up?"

"We are going to a party at the Roadhouse. Brad's back in town and Bev got a bunch of us together and we are going to throw him a Welcome Home party."

I looked at her and waited for her to lay the second part on me; the part where she would tell me that we were over and it was time for her to get on with her life with Brad. Instead she ran through who would be there and how much fun it was going to be to see a lot of the people we had lost touch with over the years.

That night and for the next two she destroyed me in the bedroom and again it left me wondering if she was being so good to me out of guilt for what she had been doing or if she was just giving me something so I would have good memories when she was gone.

We were not the first to arrive at the bar and when we got there we found that the first arrivals had put several tables together. We sat down, ordered drinks and made some general conversation with the others at the table. After a bit Patty led me out onto the dance floor and we danced to the music furnished by the juke box.

It would get a little livelier when the live band started at seven, but I relished dancing with Patty to the slow tunes from the box. She felt good in my arms and I wanted to make the most of what I figured was going to be my last night with her.

We were back at the table when Brad came in. He came over to the tables and remembering the manners my parents taught me I stood up as he approached and when he offered me his hand I took it and said:

"Welcome home."

"It's good to be back."

Patty had also stood and Brad hugged her and then stepped back, looked at her, and like he hadn't seen her in years said:

"God, but don't you look good."

The smile she gave him would have melted a stone statue. The band had set up and as they played their first number Brad asked me if I would mind if he danced with my wife. Both he and Patty looked at me like maybe they expected me to say no, but I said:

"Sure, but remember - I know your past history and I'll be expecting you to bring her back."

Brad just gave me a wolfish grin and led Patty out onto the dance floor.

More people showed up and soon there was a good party atmosphere going. I tried to treat it as any other party. I danced with some of the other girls there and Patty danced with one or two other guys, but aside from an occasional dance with me most of her dances were with Brad.

As the night progressed and the alcohol took effect, things loosened up. I noticed, and I'm sure that others did also, that Brad's hands had moved down and were on Patty's ass as he pulled her into him on the slow numbers and Patty made no effort to stop him. I noticed one or two glances in my direction from some of the other people at the table, but I pretended both not to notice the glances or what was taking place on the dance floor.

During one slow number I saw Brad and Patty move to the darkest part of the dance floor and while slowly swaying to the music they kissed. I almost got up and left at that point, but at the last second I said, "Bullshit! I'm not going to make it easy on them. Patty is going to have to tell me."

Almost as if my thoughts had crossed the space between us, Brad pulled away from Patty and walked over to me.

"Look Rob, I don't want any hard feelings over this, but Patty is mine and she always has been. I just wanted to be up front about this. Patty is leaving with me tonight."

I looked past him to Patty who was still standing on the other side of the dance floor looking toward us and the smile on her face damn near killed me. I just shrugged, turned away from him and took a sip of my drink. Everyone at the table had heard what Brad said and most of them looked away out of embarrassment and I saw pity in the eyes of the few that did look my way. I'd finish my drink and then leave. I WOULD NOT just get up and walk away with my tail between my legs.

Brad walked back to Patty, kissed her and then Patty took him by the hand and led him back to the table. I was just getting ready to stand up and leave when I saw Patty take off the gold chain with the locket on it and drop it in Brad's beer. She put her right foot up on a chair, took off the ankle chain and dropped it in his beer on top of the locket. He looked at her astonished as she walked over to me and said:

"Come on lover, I'm ready to leave."

I looked at her dumbfounded and said, "With me?"

"Who else lover? Come on. I've got an itch that I need you to scratch."

I looked from her to Brad who was sitting there with a stunned look on his face and then back to Patty who said:

"Well come on lover, let's go."

As I was pulling out of the parking lot Patty asked, "What was with that lame ass "with me?" when I said I was ready to go?"

"I was expecting you to leave with Brad and in fact he had just finished telling me that you would be leaving with him."

"I know. I stood there and watched him do it."

"And I noticed that you were smiling when he did it."

"I was. I was smiling because I knew he was making an ass of himself in front of everyone at the table and that he was in for a big surprise when it was time for me to leave."

She saw the look on my face and she said, "You honestly thought

I would leave with him?"

"Yes I did."

"You don't know me any better than that?"

"I guess maybe I don't when it comes to that. With everything I did know I was almost sure that you would be leaving with him."

"With everything you knew?"

"Come on Patricia Ann, don't go and play stupid on me here. You know full well that the reason we got married wasn't because of any deep passion that you had for me. True, I was, and still am, hung up on you, but you were up front with me about the fact that your heart was Brad's and when he came back you would be going back to him. Well, he is back and he has been back for a while and you have been seeing him for at least three weeks and hiding it from me. So tonight he tells me that you are leaving with him and while he is telling me that you are watching and smiling. Just what the hell else would I think?"

"Oh shit! You knew?"

I told her about stopping by the house and what I'd seen and heard; about following her the next day and what I had thought about her stopping with her co-workers and her Avon parties.

"And you've spent three weeks living with it. Oh God baby, I'm so sorry. I wish you would have said something. It must have been an absolute hell for you."

"It was. I went to that party tonight just knowing that it was over for us and then Brad pounded the last nail in the coffin lid. It was only pride that kept me from getting up and walking out as soon as he finished talking. I just would not let all those people at the table see me slinking off."

"I really made a mess of things didn't I? What can I do to make it up to you?"

"Maybe a start would be to tell me what the hell you have been up to these last three weeks and what was the deal with the necklace and ankle bracelet. And what about that sexy black thong that I've never seen before? Well, maybe not everything about the last three weeks. If you were fucking him I'd rather not hear about that."

"Ouch! I guess I deserved that. He never got to me baby, I promise you that. He tried; he tried hard and I led him on but he never got what belongs to you and only you. I swear. He gave me the necklace and ankle bracelet to wear so that they would mark me as his. The thong was to light your fire when we got home."

"So just what were you doing?"

"I was screwing with his mind. He had been back in town for a couple of weeks and apparently had asked around and found out where we lived and where we worked. He gambled that I would be home and that you would be at work on Columbus Day. When he rang the doorbell and I opened the door he threw open his arms, stepped forward hugged me and then kissed me. He said, "I'm back baby" and then he tried to kiss me again. I pushed him away. Then he started sweet talking me.

"The asshole had honestly thought he was going to walk into our home and I was going to rush off to bed with him. I asked him where he got off thinking I would be happy to see him after he split, told his mother not to tell me where he was and then hadn't once tried to contact me in over four years. He told me that it was all a gigantic misunderstanding and if I would just let him explain I would see that I was always on his mind and realize that he always meant to come back to me.

"Quite frankly, I did want to hear all about why he had dumped me so I invited him in and we sat out by the pool and talked. He gave me a song and dance about how he had told his mother what he had because he was still pissed at me because of our argument and he was going to let me stew for a couple of weeks. He called her back after a couple of weeks and told her she could tell me where he was and then he told her he was going to send me the money so I could join him and that is when his mother told him that we had gotten married. Then he told me that he knew that I'd only married you out of spite. But now he was back. He really thought that I would be overjoyed and he really did expect to be back between my legs before the day was over.

"That is when I decided to screw him over. I told him that he was right, that I had only married you to spite him, but that didn't change the fact that I was married and that I was not going to cheat on you. I told him that I couldn't get back with him until I ended it with you. Then I told him that he needed to leave before you got home and he got me to agree to have lunch with him the next day.

"I did meet him for lunch and told him that I wanted to be with him but that I would not do anything until you and I were legally separated. I did meet him after work for drinks and I did let him kiss me a couple of times, but every time he tried to get fresh with his hands I slapped them away and told him he would just have to wait. I kept telling him that I had to make sure that I would be okay financially when we broke up and it was taking me time to move some things and arrange some others.

"Then Bev told me she was going to do the welcome home party for Brad and I told Brad that I was finally ready and that I would let you know at the party and then I'd leave with him. He gave me the locket and the ankle bracelet and asked me to wear them at the party as a sign that I was his. Then at the party I told him that I had chickened out and that I couldn't face you and I asked him to tell you that I would be going home with him. I knew he would do it in front of everyone and then I would come over and make him look like a total dumb shit.

"I didn't know that you knew he was back and that I was talking to him. I thought you would be too stunned by what he said and you would sit there and stare at him like he was from another planet and then I would come up and make him look like a fool. It never occurred to me that you might just get up and leave. I'm sorry baby; I never meant to put you through what I put you through."

"Forget that I came home and saw you. Did it never occur to you that Bev or someone else we know might say to me that Brad was back and given your past history with him ask me how I felt about your spending time with him? Or maybe say something like "Brad is back. Are you and Patty going to be all right?" There are a hundred different ways I could have found out and all of them would have had the same bad effect on me because the bottom line would always be that way back you told me that you were Brad's and that you would go back to him when he came back. And in the last four years you never told me any different. I've spent our entire married life looking over my shoulder and praying that I would never see him again. Oh yes Patty, the last three weeks have indeed been a hell for me."

"I guess wasn't thinking too clearly about other possibilities. I just wanted to shove it up that arrogant asshole's ass. Can you forgive me?"

"What about the big increase in our sex life? Was it because you were feeling guilty?"

"Oh God no baby, it was because I'd just left a complete asshole and I was so glad to be home with you. I guess I screwed up there too. I don't think I've ever told you just how damned glad I am that I am yours. When I lost the baby and you started talking divorce to set me free I looked at what we had and realized that I had accidentally ended up with the right guy.

"I don't think I ever told you what my argument with Brad was about. He wanted to go down to Florida on spring break and I told him I wasn't going to go and so he took off in a snit. So there I was. On the one hand a guy who took off after a stupid thing like an argument over what to do over spring break and on the other a guy who put his life on hold to help out a friend and who did it fully expecting to be eventually dumped. It was a no-brainer lover; I wasn't about to let you get away. I guess I could have done a better job of letting you know that. I'll make it up to you baby, I promise you that."

As I pulled into the driveway Patty said, "I meant what I said about having an itch that I need you to scratch. Are you going to help me out with that lover?"

I parked and shut off the ignition and then looked at her. After several seconds I smiled and said:

"Race you to the bedroom."

The End

-
-
-
-
-
-
-
-

Ralph's Slut

-
-
-
-
-
-
-

I have worked for the same company for almost ten years. With the exception of the first year and a half when I was hit on by everyone, including the seventeen-year old kid in the mailroom, I have been pretty much left alone. Once the office Don Juans figured out that I was a married woman who didn't play around, the serious passes stopped and things around the office settled into harmless flirting and some kidding around. I did get a tad carried away at a couple of office Christmas parties, but it never went past some french kissing and a quick feel or two so it came as a big surprise to me when all of a sudden the office wolves were back in force. They were not only after me hot and heavy, but they seemed to think that I would be receptive.

Receptive I was not. I was flattered by all the attention I was getting, what forty-year-old woman with four kids wouldn't be, but it wasn't attention that I sought or wanted. One night after a couple of weeks of fighting off the heavy passes, I stopped at a local lounge with some people from work. I had a couple of drinks and I danced with a few of the guys. I was on the dance floor with Herb when he suddenly cupped my breast and whispered, "What say you and me go out into the parking lot for some backseat action?"

I pulled away from him and slapped him across the face as hard as I could. He gave me an angry look, "What the fuck is wrong with you Mickey?"

"What's wrong with me? What's wrong with you is the question. Where do you get off grabbing feels of me and trying to hustle me into the parking lot like some tramp?"

"If the shoe fits, wear it."

"What does that mean?"

"Look baby, if you are going to say on your web site that you like to fuck around, you shouldn't be surprised when guys want to take you up on it."

"Web site? I don't have a web site."

"Don't give me that crap Mickey. It's you, plain as day it's you. There isn't any doubt at all."

"I'm telling you that I do not have a web site and I don't have any idea of what you are talking about."

Herb gave me a long look and then said, "Okay, if that's how you want to play it. Come on. We'll go back to the office, I'll pull it up and then we will see what you have to say."

Curiosity got the best of me and so I told him to lead the way.

We walked across the street to the office, took the elevator to our floor and I followed him to his office. I watched as he brought his computer up and logged onto the Net and then clicked on Favorites.

"We'll go to yesterday's posting first." And he clicked on a URL for something and entered his user name and password. He clicked on a few more things and then we came to a screen that said, "Welcome and then he scrolled down a list until he came to "Horny Forty" and he clicked on it. He got a screen that said that said "Horny Forty" and underneath that was a thing that said STORY.

"Here she is again, my hot slut wife. Not bad for being forty and the mother of four. She loves to suck cock and take it up the ass. Her favorite things are to fuck other men while I watch and gang bangs - the more the merrier. To see more of her go to..." And it gave a URL for a site.

Herb scrolled down and I saw five pictures of me. I knew they were of me because I recognized the little butterfly tattoo that Ralph had talked me into getting and I recognized the photos as being ones that we had taken in the bedroom one night when we were fooling around with a new digital camera. There was no face so no one could possibly know that it was me, at least not unless they had seen me naked. I looked at Herb and said, "What makes you think that's me?"

"Let's go to your site." And he clicked on the link and a screen came up. Herb clicked on members, entered a password and as the screen filled my jaw dropped. It was me all right, in all my naked glory and doing things that no man but my husband was ever supposed to see. Pictures of me with a cock in my mouth. Pictures of me smiling into the camera holding my tits like I was offering them to the viewer. Pictures of me fingering myself. Pictures of me holding my pussy lips open. Pictures of me with cum on my face, with cum leaking out of my ass and with a cum filled pussy. And last, but by no means least, pictures of me being fucked in my ass and pussy all the while looking into the camera and smiling.

Stunned, I sat down on the chair next to Herb's desk and weakly asked, "Who else knows about this?"

"My guess would be everyone in the building. I know that everyone on this floor has it on their Favorites since Steve found it on the Net. You still saying that it's not you?"

"How can I? It is pretty obvious that it is me. The problem is that I don't know anything about it. Oh, I know where the pictures came from. My husband bought a digital camera and we played around with it in the bedroom, but those were supposed to be personal - no one was ever supposed to see them. God damn him! The miserable rotten bastard had no right to do this to me."

As I stared at the screen my blood began to boil as I thought of what I was going to do to Ralph when I got home and castration would be the least of it.

Herb interrupted my thoughts, "So none of this is true, I mean about the gangbangs and that stuff?"

I just looked at him as an idea formed in my mind. "The gangbang part isn't true and neither is the part about him watching me with other men, but the rest of it is pretty much on the money."

I looked at Herb as I decided what I was going to do to Ralph and then I said, "How do you feel about helping me get back at my asshole of a husband?"

"What do you mean?"

"You still want to get me on your backseat?"

Herb swept everything off his desk and onto the floor, "No. I don't want to wait for as long as it would take us to get there."

Herb's cock was the first one that I had seen since marrying Ralph almost twenty years ago. Herb wasn't as long as Ralph, but he was a good bit thicker. As I took his cock in my hand he said, "I want your ass" and I said no.

"Not this time. You are too thick for us to rush it. When I take you in my ass I want to be more relaxed and able to take more time than we have right now."

I knew that I had just told him that there would be a next time, but I didn't care. I was pretty sure that there were going to be a lot of 'next times' and not just with Herb. No sir, if Ralph wanted to put me on the Internet and tell the world that his wife was a slut, as a loving wife I couldn't let him be a liar, now could I?

Herb's cock was already hard when I took it in my hands. I knelt down in front of him and licked the head and then I licked it down to the ball sac and then back up to the head. Then I took him in my mouth and sucked on him until I felt him start to throb and I grabbed his ass cheeks and pulled him to me as he erupted in my mouth. I licked him clean and sucked on him until he was hard again and then I stood up, pulled off my panties and lay down on his desk. Herb lifted my legs up and placed them on his shoulders and as he began to work himself into me he said, "Oh God baby, you wouldn't believe how long I've wanted to do this."

Driving home I thought about everything that I'd found out. The most interesting thing was that I had enjoyed Herb. I didn't feel guilt over my infidelity; in fact I'd enjoyed it so much that after he had cum in me I had sucked him hard again and then had bent over his desk so he could take me from behind. I was tempted to go for a hat trick, but that would have put me home too late and I wasn't ready to have it out with Ralph yet. I was still thinking on how I was going to do that. Before Herb and I walked back to the lounge I made him promise to keep what we had done a secret until I could figure out how I wanted to handle things. He promised that he would in exchange for my promise that he could have my ass. "Deal," I said, and then I told him to get us a room for Thursday.

"No need for that sweetie. My apartment is just five minutes from here."

As I pulled into my drive and hit the garage door opener I thought to myself, "Ralph, you have no idea of what you have unleashed."

When I went to work the next day I set out to become what Ralph said I was. Over the next six weeks I fucked every man that I worked with. I sucked their cocks, I gave them my pussy and I took them up my ass. I did them two at a time, three at a time and if I could have figured out how I would have done them four or five at a time. In addition I had taken on Herb as an unofficial steady boyfriend and I fucked him whenever he wanted me and he wanted me a lot. Ralph took a two-day trip out of town and Herb brought a bunch of guys over to the house and I had my first really large gangbang. Eleven guys had me that night and I am almost ashamed to admit how big a slut I was. I actually had two cocks in my pussy at one time and I had never felt so full. For me the high point of the evening was when Ralph called me. I had one cock in my ass, one cock in my pussy and two guys were sucking my tits as I talked to him and it was all I could do not to scream out and thank him for making it possible. That gangbang was practice for my confrontation with Ralph.

Ralph plays poker with six friends every Thursday night. They rotate the games and last night the game was at our house. I had been waiting six weeks for Ralph's turn in the rotation to come up. Normally I would leave the house and go shopping or catch a movie, but last night I had stayed home. I let the game get started and about an hour into it I came into the dining room wearing the sluttiest outfit that I could come up with. Low cut blouse, extremely short skirt, no bra or panties and the highest heels that I owned.

"You guys ready for a break?"

I saw seven sets of eyes glued to me and Ralph's jaw drop to the floor. I had set my laptop on the buffet and I already had it hooked to the phone line. I picked it up and set it on the dining room table and turned it on.

"Here's tonight's entertainment boys."

I went through all the steps to connect to my site on the net and when the photos had loaded I scrolled through them.

"How about that one?" and I pointed to the screen. "Don't I look good with a cock in my mouth? How about this one where I have a cock in my ass? Or this one with cum all over my face? These pictures give you guys any ideas?"

Ralph's six buddies looked from Ralph to me and then back at Ralph.

"Hey, don't be wasting your time looking at him. I'm the one with three available holes. Who wants to be first?"

I looked around at Ralph's friends and they kept looking nervously at him. I walked over to Ben who was the closet to Ralph and I knelt down in front of him and started to open his fly.

"Don't mind Ralph. He's already told the world that I'm a slut, right Ralph? See there on the screen where it says that I like to fuck other guys while he watches? And did you catch the part where he says that I love gangbangs? Well, there are six of you and to me that qualifies as enough for a gangbang."

By then I had Ben's cock out and I took it in my mouth and

began sucking on it. Out of the corner of my eye I saw Ralph and his face was red, whether from anger, shame or embarrassment I didn't know, but then I didn't much care either. I took my mouth off Ben's cock and stood up. I stepped out of my skirt, took my blouse off and tossed it on the floor, "All right boys, you want Ralph's slut here on the table, or do you want to move it to the bedroom?"

It turned out that they wanted both. We started on the table and after about an hour we took it to the bedroom and it was four in the morning before they were done with me. As they were leaving I told them I would be available for all their poker games and all they had to do was call me and let me know when and where. Ralph had disappeared sometime during the first hour and he must have left the house because he wasn't there when I staggered into the bathroom to soak in a tub full of hot water. He wasn't there when I woke up at noon and it is coming up on three in the afternoon and there is still no sign of him. I have no idea of where we will go from here. We may stay together or we may not - that will be strictly up to him. I'm not as mad at him now as I was when I first found out what he had done, but that is because I found out that I like being a slut - I like having lots of cocks to play with and that is what Ralph is facing. If he can live with the slut he created, fine! If he can't - well, that's just too damned bad.

The End

-
-
-
-
-
-
-

Sally Goes to The Theatre

-
-
-
-
-
-
-

For me, the day started out bad and got progressively worse. The clock didn't go off when it was supposed to and when I woke up I was already half an hour late for work. I skipped breakfast and with only a cup of black coffee for sustenance I jumped in my car only to find that the battery was dead. It cost me $55 to get the service station to send over a guy to give me a jump-start and when I finally got down town I couldn't find a place to park. I had to settle for one of the rip-off parking lots that hosed me $30 for the day. In the elevator on the way up to the 16th floor I rehearsed my excuses for being late, but I fully expected to have my butt reamed regardless of what I said so I was pleasantly surprised when my boss caught me coming off the elevator and greeted me with:

"John! Thank God you're here. Come into my office."

As I followed him to his office I thought things might be looking up, but that hope was dashed as soon as the door closed behind us.

"The client called and is very unhappy with the proposal we sent. You have to fly out there this afternoon and see what we can do to salvage the account. Mellisa has your tickets and itinerary, and John - don't fuck this up. If we lose Johnson heads will roll."

Great I thought, just fucking great! If we lose the account, and it sounds as if we already have, and I'm the last guy to have talked to the client, guess who will get the blame. Add to that the fact that I'm terrified of flying and that my wife has been waiting two months to see the play I'm supposed to take her to see tonight, and I could see my entire life going to hell in a hand basket.

I found Mellisa, the bosses' secretary, and got my tickets and travel schedule and noticed that my luck was still running true to form - coach instead of business class or first class. Mellisa noticed my expression and said:

"Sorry John. That is all that was available on such short notice."

I gave her a weak smile and said, "Don't sweat it Mel. I'll let you make it up to me some time. You can buy me a drink if I survive this mess."

I sat down at my desk and grabbed the phone and called home knowing that the conversation I was about to have was not going to be pleasant. When Sally answered I told her what happened and asked her to pack me a bag and meet me at the airport.

"John, you can't do this to me," she yelled, "It took me three months to get the tickets for tonight's show and I've waited for the last two months for tonight to get here."

And then I did a bad thing. The day's frustrations had built up in me and I lost it.

"I don't give a rat's fuck about that goddamn play! My fucking career is on the line here and if I don't pull this off I'm going to be out of a job and I'm here to tell you that jobs that pay eighty grand a year don't grow on trees. Now please pack me that fucking bag and meet me at the airport."

There was silence on the other end of the phone for several moments and then in a very controlled voice Sally said, "You'll get your fucking bag and maybe a few other things you didn't bargain for." She hung up.

<<O>>

I was at the gate nervously pacing back and forth because it was only ten minutes until flight time and Sally hadn't shown up yet. She arrived just as they made the last call for boarding and without a word she tossed me the bag. I went to kiss her, but she stepped back and said:

"We don't have time for things like that, you have to rush off and save your precious job."

This pissed me off and so instead of trying to reason with her I just turned and boarded the aircraft. As luck would have it, bad luck of course, I got a window seat on the terminal side of the aircraft and I could see Sally watching from the window as the plane pushed back. I saw a man I didn't recognize walk up next to her, put his arm around her and then the two of them turned and walked away. With a sinking feeling in my heart I settled into my cramped seat and wondered what else God had in store for me. I didn't have long to wait to find out as the speaker system came alive.

"This is the Captain speaking. We are experiencing some erratic indications on our engine instruments and we are returning to the gate. I apologize for the inconvenience, but your safety is our primary concern. I'll keep you informed."

Five minutes after getting back to the gate the speaker squawked:

"This is the Captain. The problem is a little more serious than we thought and the aircraft is going to have to be taken to the maintenance hangar. Operations tells us that there will be another aircraft available in forty-five minutes so we are asking you to deplane at this time."

Once off the airplane I got to a pay phone and called the office to let them know the situation and then I decided to get myself a drink. I entered one of the small airport bars and was just about to sit down when I saw Sally and the man who had put his arm around her sitting at a table. I probably should have just gone over there and surprised them, but something made me move to where I could keep an eye on them, but where they might not notice me. I ordered a scotch on the rocks, but before the drink arrived, Sally and the man got up to leave. I threw a five on the table and got up to follow them. I don't know if my tailing techniques were all that good, or they were just too wrapped up in themselves to notice me, but I was able to follow them out to the rear corner of the short term parking lot where they got into a late model Ford Taurus.

I didn't see Sally's Mustang anywhere so I figured that the man must have driven her to the airport. I stood there aware that they were about to drive off and I would be unable to follow and I had just about decided to step out in front of them when I saw Sally lean over and disappear from view. From the way the man's head went back and his hands gripped the steering wheel I guessed that Sally was sucking his cock. With both of them distracted I gambled that I could move closer without being noticed and I eased my way forward until I could see Sally's head bobbing up and down in the man's lap. In only a few minutes (Sally is very good at giving head) the man took his hands from the steering wheel and put them on the back of Sally's head and held her in place while he came in her mouth. A minute later Sally sat up and wiped her mouth with the back of her hand, the man started the car, and they drove off. Somewhere along the way my decision to step out in front of them and stop them had flown away and I just stood there and watched the taillights disappear.

<<O>>

Back in the terminal, I was informed that my flight would be leaving in five minutes and that I'd better hurry on board. I spent the entire flight sitting in my seat and staring out the window and seeing Sally's head bobbing up and down in the man's lap and wondering how long she had been screwing around on me. I'd always thought we had a good marriage and had cared for each other. Sure we had problems, but what marriage didn't? The sex was still good for both of us, or at least I thought it was. I know it was good for me, but had she been faking it? Was that what this was all about?

I stumbled around in a fog the whole time I was in Boston. I don't even remember what I said to the client, but whatever it was it was good enough to save the account. The only thing I remember about the trip was my phone call to Sally when I arrived at the hotel, actually two phone calls, mine to her and hers to me. As soon as I'd checked in at the hotel I'd called Sally to let her know where she could reach me and then I asked her what she was doing.

"I'm getting ready to go to the play tonight," she said.

I said, "I thought that you didn't like to go to those things alone?"

There was a moment's silence and then Sally said, "I'm not going alone."

This time the silence was on my end of the line and then I asked, "Who are you going with?" Sally told me that she was going with someone she worked with and I asked; "Do I know her?"

Another moment of silence, this one longer than the first, and then she said, "It's not a her, it's a him. His name is Sam."

I don't know why I said what I did, it just rushed out of my mouth like it had a will of its own, "Is he the same guy you sucked off in the parking lot?"

This time there was a very long silence during which the image of Sally with her head in the man's lap, and her wiping her mouth with the back of her hand danced in my head. And then, almost defiantly, Sally said, "Yes!"

No 'how did you know?" or "I'm sorry" or anything else, just a defiant "Yes!" Stunned, by both my question and her answer, I just held the phone without speaking until I was finally able to utter a single "Oh" and hang up the phone. I spent the next four hours staring at the walls of the hotel room and wondering why God had chosen that particular day to shit all over me. The phone rang, dragging me out of the pit of despair I was wallowing in, and I answered it to find out that he wasn't done fucking over me yet.

"Hello," I said and then I heard Sally say, "Oh good. I was afraid you might have gone to bed and turned off the phone."

I looked at the bedside clock and saw that it was just past midnight, "What is it Sally?"

"You hung up on me earlier before I could say anything and I wanted to know what your slavish attention to your job cost you. When you let me know you weren't going to take me to the play I started calling around to find someone who would. Sam is the only one I could find who was free for the evening and when I asked him if he would take me he laughed and said he couldn't. He said I was a married woman and he only dates women he can take to bed. Since you had just screamed at me that you didn't, in your own words, "Give a rat's fuck about that goddamned play" and I was in a pretty pissed off mood I told him that if that was his price, I'd pay it. He didn't believe me and so I told him that if he drove me to the airport I would give him his first installment as soon as you left. Here, listen."

I suddenly heard a squish, squish sound.

Sally said, "What you just heard is the sound of Sam's cock sliding back and forth in my hot, wet pussy. This is the second time he has fucked me tonight and since he is staying over he may even fuck me a few more times. I know for sure that it will be at least once more - when we wake up in the morning. Also, he has asked me out for dinner tomorrow and if you are not home by then I'll probably go out with him and he'll fuck me again. Work hard John. Suck up to your boss and the client. Save your precious career." And she hung up.

As I said, the rest of my stay in Boston is a bit hazy and I don't even remember getting back on the airplane to fly home. That I might have done something right did not begin to dawn on me until I walked into the office to the cheers and hand clapping of my fellow workers. I'd gone straight to the office from the airport more because I couldn't face going home than for any other reason. The boss took me into his office, shook my hand, and thanked me for my efforts in saving the account, "You're the only one who could have done it," he told me and then he said there would be a sizeable bonus on my paycheck. Then he said:

"Go on home. Take a couple of days off and you and Sally can spend some time chasing each other around the house."

Yeah, right, I thought.

<<O>>

I turned onto our street just in time to see Sally get into the same Ford Taurus I'd seen at the airport and drive away. Once inside the house I dropped my bag on the floor and headed for the liquor cabinet and made myself a strong drink. Sally had figured as much because there was a note taped to the door of the cabinet;

"John - If you get home before I get back, call me on my cell phone and let me know you are home."

Why, I thought, so you can let me listen in again as you cheat on me? I read the note twice and then I wadded it up and threw it into the wastebasket. I spent the next couple of hours nursing a scotch on the rocks and wondering what I was going to do. Just after eleven a car pulled into the drive and parked behind my car and I watched through the bedroom window as Sally started to get out. The driver reached over and grabbed her and pulled her back in. A couple of minutes passed as they sat there, probably talking, and then Sally again started to get out of the car. Again the driver grabbed Sally and it looked like she was struggling to pull loose and I almost talked myself into going out there, but at the last moment I said:

"Fuck it. She made her bed, let her lie in it."

I took a sip of my scotch and continued to watch. Sally stopped trying to get away from the man and a moment later her head disappeared below the dash. It was almost five minutes before her head came back up and I watched as she wiped her mouth with the back of her hand just as she had in the airport parking lot. There seemed to be some more talking and then Sally and the driver got out of the car, but instead of coming toward the house they got in the backseat of the car. I saw

Sally lay back and both she and the man disappeared from view and a minute later I saw both of her legs come up and began to kick in the air. I turned and walked away from the window and headed for the bed. Tomorrow was going to be a very bad day at our house.

The End

-
-
-
-
-
-
-

Teri

-
-
-
-
-
-
-

I got my reputation as a nerd early in life - before I was even out of grade school. Both of my parents were college professors and they saw to it that studious habits were deeply instilled in me. Another thing that they insisted on was a well-rounded education and so while the other kids in the neighborhood were out playing sandlot baseball or shooting hoops on some school playground I was being exposed to culture.

With my parents dragging me along, we spent entire weekends in museums. We haunted art galleries and I had to listen to endless discussions on the differences in techniques used by Manet and Monet, the brush strokes of Villbert versus the daub and smear of Rachmann. We had season tickets to the opera and the symphony. Some of it took and some of it didn't, but the result was that by the end of high school my reputation as a nerd was well established.

Also well-established was my reputation as Mr. Nice Guy. My parents had hammered at good manners and proper behavior and so my social comportment was perfect. What wasn't apparent were a few other things that they taught me, but more on that later. I dated a lot in high school, but I was still a virgin when I graduated - it was part of the 'nice guy' thing. Whether it was kissing or copping a feel, if the girl said no that was the end of it - I stopped. I know that in a lot of cases it was just part of the dance and that I could have gone farther, but to me no always meant just that - no!

Nothing much changed at college. I studied hard, made the Dean's List every term, dated and in general enjoyed the college experience to the hilt. Then about four months before graduation I met Teri. She was a four foot nine walking wet dream and I fell hopelessly in love with her. She had a reputation of being just a little on the wild side and so I was very surprised that she said yes when I asked her for a date. I guess we hit it off because we were opposites and they say that opposites attract. Whatever the reason, by the third date Teri owned me. On the third date I tried to kiss Teri for the first time and she pushed me away. "It's a little soon for this," she said, "It's only been a week since I broke up with my boyfriend and I don't know if I'm ready yet." True to form, I took no as meaning no and I made no further attempt to kiss her. At the end of the date I took her home, walked her to her door, said goodnight and then I left.

The next two days were spent cramming for midterms so it was three days before I got a chance to call Teri again. She sounded surprised to hear from me, "I didn't think you were interested in me anymore."

"Why would you think that?"

"Well, you didn't even try to kiss me goodnight when you brought me home and then I didn't hear from you for three days."

"But you said no when I tried to kiss you."

"Oh good grief. Don't you know that a girl wants the guy to work for it? If I just kissed everyone who tried to kiss me I'd have a hell of a reputation."

It didn't take Teri long to figure out that she could wrap me around her little finger. We became a steady couple, steady in that she spent two thirds of her free time with me, but she still went out with other guys. We were kissing, but any attempts I made at getting more intimate were rebuffed which is why I didn't believe any of the rumors that I heard about her. I heard some people say that she was a sure thing if you could get her to go out with you, but if that were the case I would have scored by then. I would ask her to go somewhere with me and she would tell me that she was sorry, but she had a date that night and then I would look at her with a 'kicked puppy dog look' and she would say, "Come on baby, don't be that way. A girl has to see what's out there while she is still young." I saw her point and she was spending most of her time with me so I didn't fight it.

Two months before graduation I took Teri out to a movie and on the way home she asked me to take her to a place she'd heard about and it turned out to be kind of a lover's lane. We started necking and after a bit Teri took my hands and put them on her breasts and things just went from there. We made love on the front seat and I'm ashamed to admit how quick it was, but then Teri gave me my very first blow job and got me hard again and I lasted a little longer the second time. Then Teri told me that since she had given me oral that it was only fair that I do her and while I did she played with me until I was hard again and then we moved to the back seat. We spent the entire weekend in bed and after that most of our free time was spent on any flat surface that we could find. The week of graduation, Teri told me that she was pregnant. When I told her that we had to get married she told me that she didn't feel right in trapping me into a marriage that way and that I didn't have to marry her unless I really wanted to.

We were married in a civil ceremony the week after graduation. The baby, a boy, came seven months and three weeks later. When I asked the doctor if there were any problems because of his being born premature he gave me a funny look, "Premature? I'd say he's about two weeks late."

Teri had played me for a sucker and I knew that I was not the father of the child. But I was crazy about Teri and after all she had chosen me to be her husband so I decided not to say anything and let her keep on thinking that I thought little Andy was mine.

In retrospect that was a mistake. It gave Teri the sense that she could put things over on me and over the next five years I'm sure that she did even though I never knew about it. I finally found out by accident that she was indeed putting things over on me. My job requires that I spend about three days twice a month calling on our outlets and I was scheduled to leave on one of those trips the next day. I had taken the elevator down to the parking garage and was unlocking the door to my car when I noticed what looked like damage on the left front fender. It looked like it had been run into. I was squatting down and looking at the damage when the elevator doors opened and I heard "…see Teri while Brian is gone?" The voices belonged to Mark and Stan, two guys that I worked with. They stopped at Mark's car and kept talking.

"I don't know. She's a great fuck, but she is just a little bit too wild. Sooner or later Brian is going to catch on and I don't necessarily want to go down when she does."

(Short laugh) "But going down is one of the things that she does best."

(More laughter) "Why did you stop fucking her?"

"She cut me off. I went over there one afternoon and she had two scruffy looking biker types and she was doing both of them. She told me to hurry up and get undressed, but I was reluctant to have anything to do with those guys. They looked unclean, not dirty, but unclean if you know what I mean."

"Yeah."

"So anyway, she told me to get out and not to bother coming back."

"Do you think Brian knows?"

"I wouldn't doubt it."

"Why doesn't he stop it?"

"Who knows? He's a nice guy. But in my experience nerdy nice guys are wimps. He is probably too afraid to say anything."

"Yeah, she might cut him off."

More laughing and then car doors slamming and I heard them drive off. I slowly stood up and stood there staring at the ramp they had driven up and wondered how in the hell I was ever going to be able to work with them after hearing what they said.

Dinner was quiet and when Teri asked me if anything was wrong I told her that I was just thinking about some problems at work.

"Well put them aside sweetie. You will be gone for three days so you have to come upstairs and see that I get enough to hold me until you come back."

That's something that I couldn't understand. According to Stan and Mark she was not only fucking them, but others too and yet our sex life couldn't have been better - damn near every night and usually more than once. Could they possibly have been talking about another Brian and Teri? As soon as I had the thought I knew that I was trying to go into denial; I was the only Brian that worked at the company and there were no Teri's working there either.

In the morning Teri woke me with a blow job and when I tried to pull out of her mouth so we could make love she wouldn't let me. She took her mouth off me just long enough to say, "I don't want you to forget about me while you are gone." When I came she kept sucking and licking until I was soft and the she said, "While you're away keep it in your pants. You know you won't find anybody else who is as good as I am." I was tempted to say the same to her but I didn't.

I left the house at my regular time, but I didn't catch the Interstate for Kansas City. I stopped at a Denny's and sipped coffee while I called all the outlets I was supposed to visit and told them I would be a day late in getting to them. Then I went to a Target and bought a large thermos bottle and went back to Denny's and had it filled with coffee. I got a copy of both of the daily papers and a USA Today and drove back to the neighborhood, found a place to park where I could watch the house and settled in to wait and watch.

It was a long wait and I nodded off a couple of times before a van pulled up in front of the house. It said Regal Painting on the sides and two men got out and went into my house. They didn't knock or ring the bell, they just opened the door and went in. I waited fifteen minutes and then I drove into my driveway and went into the house. I could hear them as soon as I went in the front door. Teri is very vocal during the sex act and her cries of pleasure rang through the house. I walked upstairs and stopped at the bedroom door and looked in at Teri riding the cock of one man while she was sucking on the other one. Both men were facing me and saw me at the same time. Teri's back was to me and she hadn't seen me yet. Her first clue that something was wrong was when the man in her mouth pulled out of her and the guy she was riding stopped pushing up at her. She turned to see what they were looking at and then she surprised the living hell out of me - she smiled at me! She smiled and said, "Baby, you're back. You are just in time. These guys are going to need some help."

I was stunned into silence for several moments and then I cleared my head and said, "It's time for you guys to leave."

The guy who had been getting his cock sucked said, "You got that wrong buddy. We don't leave until the lady tells us to."

Then Teri spoke up, "I don't want them to leave Brian. We were just starting to have fun."

The guy she was sitting on pushed her off him and stood up, "There you have it pal. We stay, you go."

I pointed at the bedroom door and said, "Out! Both of you and right now!"

The two of them looked at each other and then one of them said "I guess we will just have to throw him out." And they both began to walk toward me.

One of the things that my father had insisted that I learn is that violence is only for the stupid. He used to say, "I don't care what the circumstance, what the occasion, violence is not the answer. Walk away from it." And then he went on to say, "But that doesn't mean that you meekly submit. The only time violence is appropriate is when you are physically attacked. I don't mean pushed around or shoved, but when the other party is going to physically lay hands on you, hit you, pull a knife on you or something of an equally violent nature. At that time meeting violence with violence not only should be done, but must be done."

Before dad got his PHD, courtesy of the GI Bill, he spent three tours in Vietnam with Special Forces. He taught me to box and he taught me the basics of hand to hand combat. None of the high kicking, leg sweeping karate shit, but Judo and some other defensive stuff. He didn't teach me any of the offensive moves, just what I needed to defend myself. "Don't forget," he would say, "Defense properly directed is offense enough."

As the two men approached me I took off my glasses and put them in my shirt pocket and one of the guys said, "Ooh, I think he wants to fight us." Teri was screaming at us to stop, but when the first man made a move to grab me I stepped inside of his reach, took his forearm and bent it at the elbow and levered him past me headfirst into the wall (defense properly directed) and he slid to the floor like a bag of wet sand. The other guy moved in on me while I was taking care of his buddy and swung at me. I caught his arm, moved past him and twisted and he flipped over and fell on his back. I stepped on his throat and put my weight on that foot and watched his eyes bulge as his air was cut off. "I asked you to leave. Are you going now or not?" He was waving his hands and I took that as a yes and I took my foot off his throat and stepped back. "Take your friend and leave and don't you ever come back." I gathered up their clothes and tossed them at him and he got shakily to his feet and went to help his buddy stand up.

I watched them leave and then I walked out of the bedroom and headed down the stairs. Teri came running after me, "Brian, where are you going?"

"I have a business trip I'm supposed to be on, remember? That little thing I do twice a month so you can do this shit while I'm gone?"

"But we need to talk."

"No Teri, you might need to talk, but I have no interest in listening."

"Please Brian, let me explain."

"If you are still here when I get home on Friday maybe I'll listen to you, but then again, maybe I won't." And I walked out the door.

I tried to put it out of my mind during my trip, but of course that just wasn't possible. I remembered all the rumors I'd heard about Teri in college that I didn't (or wouldn't) believe. Then there was little Andy who I already knew wasn't mine, although I was determined that he would never know it. Then I wondered how many and for how long. Did I really care enough to care? Aye, there was the rub. I did care. I was still as crazy about Teri as I had been on the day that I had met her. It sounds hokey, but she made my days and my nights and I could not conceive of a life without her. But equally I couldn't conceive of a life with her as she bounced merrily along on whatever cock she could get her hands on. And what about that "I don't want them to leave" and that "I'm glad you're back, these guys are going to need some help" shit? Did she honestly think that I didn't care and that I would have said okay? Then there was little Andy. If I tossed Teri out, she would take him with her. He wasn't mine, but he was if you know what I mean. I'd been raising him and the little shit had a hold on me that I didn't want broken. And then there was work - how could I go back to that office and work with Stan and Mark? All of that stuff and more rattled around inside my head during the trip and when I got home on Friday I had no more clue as what to do than I'd had when I left for the trip.

When I got home the house was dark and I looked around, but no one was home. I went up to check the closets to see if Teri had taken her stuff and moved out. The bedroom looked like a war zone. Torn nylons on the floor, a couple of pair of heels lying around, bed sheets tangled and stains all over them. On the bedside table a box of Trojans, twelve count, lay empty on its side and I counted seven of them tied off and thrown in the wastebasket. Teri obviously hadn't spent much time being worried while I was gone.

I was in the kitchen getting myself a beer when I heard the front door open and a minute later Teri walked into the kitchen. She was wearing a short skirt, a low cut blouse and high heels. I looked her up and down, "Going out?"

"Yes. I have a date tonight. I just took Andy over to the sitters."

"So much for needing to talk."

"Hey, the way you walked out pretty much told me that we were toast."

"I could tell from the bedroom that it didn't bother you all that much."

"It's what I have done for years, I just don't have to hide it now."

"For years?"

"Yes, for years. Ever since you got the job that took you out of town."

"Why?"

"Because I like it. No, that's not right. I do it because I love it. I always have and my getting married to you was a mistake."

She saw the look that passed over my face, "Oh don't look at me like that. I didn't say I didn't love you, because I do. From the moment I met you I knew you were the man meant for me. I've never loved anyone or anything the way I love you, but love and sex are not the same thing Brian, at least not for me. Getting married was a mistake for me because I'm not the kind of girl who can be satisfied by only one cock. I knew that about myself long before I met you and I should have been smart enough to know that I wouldn't change. But I loved you and I wanted to be your wife so I convinced myself that I could make the marriage work. I was wrong."

"I'm supposed to believe you married me because I was your one and only true love instead of believing you just needed a sucker because you were pregnant with Andy?"

"Yes, I expect you to believe it because it's true. I don't have a clue as to who Andy's father was. It could have been anyone of a dozen different guys and when I got pregnant I looked at all the ones I'd been with, any one of whom would have been tickled to death to marry me, and all I saw were a bunch of irresponsible, beer chugging party animals. I wanted my child to have a good father and that was you. I know I tried to trick you into thinking Andy was yours, but I knew when he came that you were not stupid enough to believe that a healthy baby like Andy was a preemie. But you never said a word and I thought that meant that you wanted me regardless of what I'd done. Don't doubt that I love you Brian. Why else would I have stayed with you? Why else would I have kept on dating you while I was fucking every other guy who would take out his cock for me if I didn't care for you? You could have been Andy's father if you weren't such a damned nice guy. Maybe it was my fault for not making you fuck me sooner, but you were so nice and sweet that I didn't want you to think I was an easy piece of ass and so I kept waiting for you to make a move."

A horn honked out front. "I've got to go," she said as she picked her purse up off the table, "Don't wait up."

As she walked toward the front door I asked, "Are you going to fuck him?"

"Of course. Why else would a married woman go out on a date with another man?'

"But what about us?"

"If there is to be an us Brian, it will have to be with the understanding that I'm a slut, I love cock, and you will have to share me. You will get all the love, the hugs and kisses, the snuggling and cuddling and you will still own the best piece of ass in town. Again baby, don't ever doubt that I love you and only you, but other guys will still be getting into my pussy. Think about it and if you are still here when I get home we can talk some more about it." And then she left me standing there staring as the living room door closed behind her.

I had tears running down my face as I went upstairs to pack.

The End

Velma Goes to Work

We were up against it. Credit card debt was eating us up and we always seemed to be on the verge of not being able to make the house payment. It was our own fault of course, I'd had a good paying job, the money coming in was more than enough to cover our bills and like a lot of people we lived at the level of our income. But my good job had disappeared when the company I worked for was bought out and 183 of us were let go.

The only jobs I could find paid a good one third less than the one I'd had so we were automatically on the slippery slope toward bankruptcy. Finally Velma told me that she was going to get a job to get some extra money coming in. This was pretty much a kick in the teeth to me as I had been brought up to believe that the man supported the household and the woman took care of it, but that would be a moot point if we lost the house.

Velma had become a housewife without ever having had a job. Her parents had given her a good allowance and she went from high school to college to marriage so she had no saleable skills, but she was determined to try. After two months she had nothing to show for her efforts except several call backs from Burger King, McDonalds and the like, all wanting her to work 24 hour weeks with split shifts which of course she wasn't interested in.

Then one of her girl friends told her about a lounge that was looking for a few good cocktail waitresses and the only job qualifications were the ability to be able to handle yourself around a bunch of rowdy men and women and to look good in the uniform that was supplied. I wasn't too keen on the idea, but we did need the money so I told Velma that she could look into it.

Velma went to the lounge and applied for the job and when she came home that afternoon she said that the job was hers, but only on the condition that I would never come in to the lounge while she was working - any other time was okay, but never while she was on duty. The owner, a man named Cliff, told her that he did not like to hire married women because of all the trouble he'd had with jealous husbands. The uniform she would wear showed a lot of cleavage and the skirt was short and showed a lot of leg (I had a quick image of Velma in a uniform like that - slim, narrow waisted and with 38 C cup breasts she would be an attention getter).

The whole marketing strategy was to hire good-looking waitresses to attract male customers who would then sit and drink while enjoying the scenery. The problems happened when a husband would come into the lounge and then get pissed at a customer who he thought was paying too much attention to his wife. It had happened so often that Cliff had just about made up his mind to not hire any more married women. I could see that getting this job meant a lot to Velma and I'd never been much for spending time in bars anyway so I told her she could tell Cliff I'd stay away unless invited by him.

Velma started the next day. Her shift was from noon until nine, Tuesday through Saturday and she got Friday, Saturday, Sunday and Monday off on every fourth weekend. Seven months went by with Velma making some very good money, mostly in tips and then her days started to get longer and longer. At first it was until ten, then eleven, then midnight, and finally she was working until closing on some nights. She said Cliff was having a hard time finding good help and she was making good money working the extra hours to cover the shifts. I wasn't happy about her long hours, but the money was good and we were digging ourselves out of the hole.

By the end of the seventh month we had paid off two credit cards, were two months ahead on the house payments, and actually had two grand in savings. Also on the plus side our sex life had greatly improved. We went from twice a week to sometimes five and six times a week. And the way we had sex changed too. Velma had never liked having her pussy eaten, but now almost every session started with us doing a sixty-nine. Many were the nights that I'd be in bed asleep when she would get home and she would wake me up by sucking my dick and then move into a sixty-nine position and push her hot, wet pussy into my face.

Hot and wet - that was the part I couldn't figure, her pussy was always very wet when she came home. Velma told me it was because of all the sexual tension at work; the guys always hitting on her and making propositions, and all the "accidental" touching had her hot by the end of her shift. Hey! Who was I to complain? I was getting great sex, we were climbing out of debt and things couldn't have been better.

And then a developer started building houses on the vacant field behind our house. All of the construction and earth moving disturbed the field mice and so they all went looking for a new home. Several had invaded out house and for weeks I'd been setting traps and trying to control them. One day I saw one of the little rascals dart into Velma's sewing room and I went in after him. I saw him go under the closet door and when I opened the door he ran behind some shoeboxes in one corner. I took the top off one of the shoeboxes and dumped the contents on the floor and then I turned it upside down and managed to trap the little bugger under it.

After disposing of the mouse I went back to pick up the stuff I'd dumped on the floor. One of the items was a bankbook for a savings account. Out of curiosity I opened it and was surprised to see that it was for a current account and that it had a balance of $33,618.12 and that the date of the last deposit was one week ago. The rest of the papers were bank statements, addressed to Velma at the lounge, and they showed that in addition to the savings account, Velma had a checking account with a balance of $3,287.62. I knelt there stunned by the discovery and wondered just what the hell was going on. I put everything back where I found it and went into the kitchen, made myself a stiff drink and tried to figure out what to do.

That night I was parked outside the lounge at what was supposed to be Velma's regular quitting time. At 9:15 she came out the front door dressed in her street clothes and stood waiting by the curb. She waited about two minutes and then a car pulled up, Velma got in, and the car drove away. I followed it at what I hoped was a safe distance and I was not all that surprised when their destination turned out to be a motel.

It was three hours before she came out of the motel room and was driven back to the lounge to get her car. I beat her home and was in bed pretending to be asleep when she got home. She undressed and came straight to bed and I felt her lips fasten onto my cock. When she had sucked on me enough to insure that I would be awake she swung over me and pushed her hot, wet pussy into my mouth. Hot and wet, only now I knew why - the wet had come out of the head of another man's cock. Knowing that did not stop me from eating Velma out and why should it? I'd been doing it for over six months now and it hadn't hurt me yet. The sex we had that night was intense. I just could not get enough of Velma and it seemed to be all right with her.

For the next two weeks I waited outside the lounge and every night but two were the same. Velma would get off work and go to a motel with some guy and when she came home that night her cum filled pussy would always be shoved in my face.

The other two nights were a different story. On one of them she got into a van and was driven to the motel, but when she got out, four guys got out of the van with her, not one. That night when she got home, a veritable river ran out of her and into my mouth. The other time was the only time I got to see her in action. She came out of the lounge and walked out to the parking lot and got in one of the parked cars. I got out of my car and made my way to a place where I could see what was going on.

Velma was in the front seat, naked from the waist up and she was sucking a guy's cock while he played with her 38C tits. After about five minutes she pulled her head back and I saw the guys cum squirt out of the head of his cock, then he and Velma got in the back seat and I watched as he fucked her. The image of her high-heeled feet waving around in the air as his ass kept moving up and down between her legs still makes me hard.

It has been eight months since I found her savings book and once a month or so I check the balance and it continues to grow. I wondered what she was going to do with the money and how she was going to explain it to me some day.

Then last Friday I noticed a withdrawal from her savings of $31,000. Yesterday I came home from work to find a brand new Ford F-350 Super Duty Crew Cab parked in the driveway. It had a big ribbon tied around it and a card under the windshield wiper. It read:

Happy Birthday, Baby
Love,
Velma
P.S. Don't worry. I'm making enough in tips to make the payments.

I don't know, and I'm not ready to ask her why she is so hot to fuck me after being fucked by one of her customers, or what need of hers is fulfilled by having me eat their cum out of her. I only know that I am extremely turned on knowing that she is fucking other men and coming home to me. And, for right now at least, I don't want it to stop.

~~The End~~

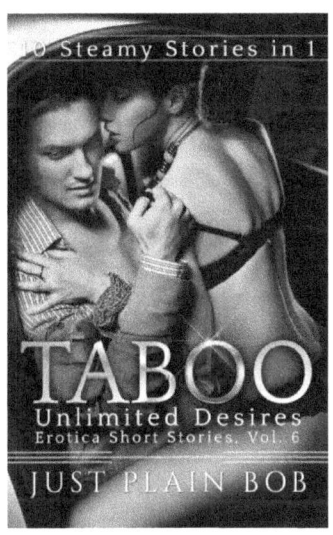

Also by this Author:

A Weird One

Becoming a Shared Husband, Vol. 1 –

(Suck Me)

Becoming a Shared Husband, Vol. 2 –

(Husbands Who Stray)

Becoming a Shared Husband, Vol. 3 –

(Get even!)

Becoming a Shared Couple, Vol. 1 –

(Steamy Swingers)

Erotica Short Stories, Vol. 1

(Taboo Desires)

Erotica Short Stories, Vol. 2

(Nasty Steps)

Erotica Short Stories, Vol. 3

(Married But...)

Erotica Short Stories, Vol. 4

(Sizzling 10)

From the Author

If you enjoyed any of my books then please share the love and promote my books in Amazon.

If you write me a review and send me an email I will send you a free book, or many.
(Just know that these emails are filtered by my publisher.)

Good news is always welcome.

One Last Thing, For Kindle Readers...

When you turn the page, Kindle will give you the opportunity to rate this book and share your thoughts on Facebook and Twitter. If you enjoyed my writings, would you please take a few seconds to let your friends know about it? Because... when they enjoy they will be grateful to you and so will I.

Thank You!

An Open Letter from Just Plain Bob

A message for those who like my stories, those who hate my stories, those who are indifferent and those who have yet to make up their minds.

I have often stated that I really don't care what others think about my stories, that I write for my own enjoyment and then I offer to share. If you like my stories fine and if you don't, also fine since I have already satisfied my target audience - me!

It is human nature to strive to get better. If you take up bowling your first games are going low scoring, but you will work and practice to get better and as your average climbs you may forget the game where you had three gutter balls and shot an eighty-six, but that game is still there in your past.

Your first time on the golf course you shot an eighty on the front nine, but did you settle for that being your game or did you work to improve? You may eventually get a three handicap, but that nine hole eighty is still there as part of your past.

When you hired in at your job did you say, "Cool, I got it made" and do nothing more than what you barely had to do or did you go to work thinking that, "Someday I'm going to be running this place." You might never climb that high, but human nature says that you are going to at least try.

It is the same with authors who write stories and post them on sites like Literotica. Their first stories might not be all that good, but comments and feedback along with a desire to get better drive them toward putting out a better product or to at least try.

I'm no different. My first stories might not have been all that great, but they are still there on the hard drive. I like cheating wife stories and five years ago I found my first adult site that catered to cheating wife stories. It was a pay site, but it had a policy of giving a free lifetime membership to anyone who submitted five stories to the site. How hard can that be I said to myself as I sat down and fired up the word processor and went to work.

I sent my five stories in and sat back to enjoy my free membership and a funny thing happened. I started getting feedback, most of it positive, and I became hooked. I started cranking out more stories. The site I was sending my stories to had seven categories:

Bisexual
Cream Pie

Groups
I Watch
Gang Bang
Racial
SM/BD

I know nothing about bisexual or SM/BD and I had no interest in Groups so all the stories I wrote I tailored for the four remaining categories:

Cream Pie
I Watch
Gang Bang
Racial.

I turned out eight stories a month, two for each category, which means that after five years I have over 120 stories in each of those categories and they are all still on the hard drive.

A year ago I received an email asking me why I never posted stories on Literotica. The answer? I didn't know about Lit. I pulled it up, liked what I saw, and started sending in stories to it. All new stories? No, not hardly, not with over 400 stories sitting on the hard drive. Maybe one new story for each fifteen or so old ones. The newer ones are better, at least I think they are and I have received some feedback that leads me to believe that others think so too, and I will continue to write new ones.

But I am still going to recycle what is on the hard drive, stories that were written specifically to fit the four categories. That means that those of you who hate cream pie stories still have eighty or so to look forward to. Ditto for those who call me a racist; you will get another seventy or so interracial stories.

Those who hate wimps will only see about fifty more of those because the stories I sent to the I Watch category were split 50/50 between what some call wimps and some call "real men." Why the 50/50 split? It came from listening to the readers. I would get feedback asking me why all the men in my stories were hard asses. "In real life men are more forgiving, especially if it is the first indiscretion." So I would write stories with forgiving husbands and boyfriends and then the next batch of feedback would say, "Why are all your husbands spineless wimps" and I'd write stories that went back the other way.

Eventually I came to realize that I was wasting my time - there was no way I could write a story that would satisfy everybody and that is when I adopted my philosophy of writing for my own enjoyment and then offering to share.

As far as the gangbang stories? Well, what can I say? Gangbangs are gangbangs and there are still eighty or so of them to go.

The bottom line is that Literotica readers are going to see more of my old stories than my new ones. If I'm still around three or four years from now it will probably go the other way, more new than old.

I feel the need to respond to some of the comments and emails I have received. By far the largest percentage comes from people who say, "You are an asshole because all women are not whores and sluts and that's all you make them out to be."

Next most common is, "You must really hate women you sick fuck."

"You must be a wimp because all the men in your stories are wimps" is up there in the top ten along with, "Why don't you give it a rest and go crawl off in a hole somewhere."

There is a lot more, but I'm only going to address those four and in reverse order.

I won't stop and go crawl in a hole because I am enjoying the hell out of what I am doing and remember what I said, I am doing this for MY OWN ENJOYMENT and then I offer to share. Some obviously like my sharing with them and so I will continue to do so. No one is holding a gun to a reader's head and telling them they must click on a Just Plain Bob story or die. It is a conscious choice on the reader's part to move that mouse and click on that story.

When a man finds out he has a cheating wife or girlfriend there are only a limited number of ways he can handle it. If he loves her he can forgive, try to forget and try to hold on and somehow make things work. He can turn his back on her, walk away and get on with his life. The third option is to take revenge.

According to a good portion of those who send me feedback the first and second options are proof that the men are wimps. If the man takes the third option he is still considered a wimp if he doesn't do some sort of physical damage to the woman and her lover. These readers believe that the only way not to be a wimp is to kill, maim and destroy everything in sight. Doing that however, will invariably get the man throw in jail and that is why it so rarely happens in real life.

In real life most revenge takes place in the man's head when he says to himself, "I should have _____ (fill in the blank) the fucking cunt!" I know this because I have been there and done that (see The Dark Trilogy). In my stories I try to mirror real life so kill, maim and destroy are going to be for the most part absent. Outside of some fisticuffs there will be very little physical violence in my stories. Most of my husbands are going to do what I did, what several of my friends and others that I know have done, forgive, or walk away. If this makes them wimps and me a wimp for writing the story that way, so be it.

Next is the "I must hate all women." Nothing could be farther from the truth. I love women. I lust after women. I even like whores and sluts. I have been married four times, engaged two other times (that did not end in marriage) and I have always had girlfriends between marriages. My philosophy is that women were put on this earth for me to enjoy and I'm not talking just sexually. I could sit at the mall (and have) for hours and just girl watch.

The engagements, girlfriends and three of the four marriages bring me to the #1 anti JPB comment on the list.

"You are an asshole because all women aren't whores and sluts."

Well dear reader, you can not prove that by me! I will say up front that I KNOW all women aren't whores and sluts, BUT the majority of the women in my life were. My mother ran around on my father for years while he was driving a truck for a living. My Aunt Margaret cheated regularly on my Uncle Bill, as did my Aunt Mildred on my Uncle Paul. My Aunt Betty fucked around on my Uncle Bob for years and finally left him for his brother, my Uncle Wendell. Uncle Wendell in turn caught her on her knees at his company Christmas party giving Season's Greetings to his boss.

My sister is three times divorced and each divorce came about when the then current husband caught her out spreading pollen. Both of the engagements I mentioned ended when I found out that I was not the one and only and a lot of the girls I dated between marriages never made it to engagement status for the same reason.

And that brings me to my three ex-wives. The first one, Helen (I believe I commented on her in the intro to The Dark Trilogy) had seven different lovers before I found out what was going on. I was living proof that love is blind. Ditto with my second wife. She had a secret life that she hid from me and when I found out about her brother, his friends and the gangbangs she was history.

My third marriage ended in divorce because of a different kind of cheating (and I can just imagine the outrage I am going to get over this) - she cheated on me with an idea. I was away from home on business, she was lonely, a couple of Jehovah's Witnesses knocked on the door and my wife, with nothing better to do invited them in. When I came home from my trip I found out that she had found God. On a scale that runs from TRUE BELIEVER on one end to ATHEIST on the other you will find me just to the right of AGNOSTIC and since I would not allow myself to be SAVED the marriage eventually died.

So yes, I write about sluts and whores because as everyone knows, you tend to write about the things you know. And I do like sluts and whores, just not the ones that lie to me and cheat on me.

So be forewarned - if you click on a Just Plain Bob story you will be getting sluts, whores and husbands who do not kill, maim and destroy. There are other things you will rarely find in a Just Plain Bob story. Even though I try to mirror real life my stories all take place in StoryLand. In StoryLand STDs and un-wanted pregnancies do not exist unless the author feels like they may add something to the story. Bad things do not happen in StoryLand unless the author so wills it and no amount of "You should have…" in comments and feedback will change a story already posted.

Lastly, I will touch on a truth. None of what I have written here means shit because the same readers will still read the same stories that they profess to hate and make the same comments they have always made. Knowing this, I will deliberately post stories that will have them frothing at the mouth.

It is the least I can do for an adoring public.

Thank you!

Just Plain Bob
justplainbob@awesomeauthors.org

www.ingramcontent.com/pod-product-compliance
Lightning Source LLC
Chambersburg PA
CBHW071402170626
46811CB00003B/1232